Cruel Fictions, Cruel Realities

Short Stories by
Latin American Women Writers

Cruel Fictions, Cruel Realities

Short Stories by
Latin American Women Writers

Edited and Translated by
Kathy S. Leonard

Foreword by
Ana María Shua

The Latin American Literary Review Press publishes Latin American creative writing under the series title Discoveries, and critical works under the series title Explorations.

Copyright © 1997 Latin American Literary Review Press
Library of Congress Cataloging-in-Publication Data

Cruel Fictions, cruel realities: short stories by Latin American women
    writers / edited and translated by Kathy S. Leonard.
    p.cm
    ISBN 0-935480-87-0
    1. Short stories, Spanish American–Translations into English.
    2. Spanish American fiction–20th century–Translations into English.
    3. Spanish American fiction–Women authors–Translations into
    English. 4. Cruelty in literature. I. Leonard, kathy S., 1952-.
PQ7087.E5C78 1997   97-13681
863'.0108868–dc21   CIP

Copyright Acknowledgments:
For permission to publish or reproduce the material which appears in this anthology, acknowledgment is made to the following sources:

"Corners of Smoke" by Gloria Artigas, translated by Kathy S. Leonard, first
    appeared in *The Antigonish Review* 106 (1996): 145-148.
"A Mother to be Assembled" by Inés Fernández Moreno, translated by Kathy
    S. Leonard, first appeared in *Flyway: A Literary Review* 2.2 (Fall
    1996): 74-79.
"A Profession Like Any Other" by Ana María Shua, translated Kathy S.
    Leonard, first appeared in *Puerto del Sol* 31.3 (1996): 90-97.

Cover art by Mirta Toledo.
Cover design by Connie Mathews.

The paper used in this publication meets the minimum requirements of the American National Standard for Permanence of Paper for Printed Library Materials Z39.48-1984. ∞

Printed in Canada

Acknowledgments

This project is supported in part by a grant from the Commonwealth of Pennsylvania Council on the Arts and Iowa State University.

Editor/Translator's Acknowledgments

Many people have helped to make this anthology possible. I would like to gratefully acknowledge Iowa State University for granting me a faculty improvement leave which allowed me the time to complete the manuscript. I would also like to thank the Department of Education, Cornell/Pittsburgh Consortium for awarding me a Research Fellowship/Visiting Scholar appointment to Cornell University which allowed me access to the extensive collection of Latin American materials held in Olin Library. I am indebted to the authors whose work appears in this volume, for their enthusiastic cooperation, participation, and permission to translate and include their work. Finally, I wish to thank Michael Porter, not only for his patience and support while I worked on this project, but also for reading and reviewing all materials and translations and offering helpful comments and suggestions.

Contents

Foreword
by Ana María Shua

An anthology like all the rest?

As a writer myself, I am not accustomed to writing forewords for anthologies, especially for those that include my stories. But I find this exercise to be an interesting challenge, especially since the reading of the stories in this collection gave me great aesthetic, intellectual, and political pleasure. Therefore, I would like to trace my experience while writing this foreword, from the initial proposal, to the reading of the stories, including the seductive effect they produced over me, and concluding with my final analysis.

When presented with this type of anthology, we writers have a series of questions that can only be dismissed or confirmed by a reading of the stories themselves. We ask ourselves, for example:

Will the literary as well as the ideological values of the volume be adequately protected?

Do we claim that women write a particular type of literature?

Is it enough to simply be a Latin American woman or do we also have to demonstrate it?

Does the collection contain the usual authors included in many other anthologies, those who are the most often translated because they are the best sellers, or are new authors being introduced?

Is the collection completely haphazard, guided only by the personal preference of the editor?

I will attempt to respond to these questions for the reader, just as I responded to them for myself after my first reading of *Cruel Fictions, Cruel Realities*. In my response, the qualities that distinguish this collection from others will emerge.

The position of women writers: Reasons to be distrustful

When Latin American writers are asked to contribute work for a women's anthology, our first reaction is not always positive; we often feel somewhat annoyed and distrustful. Once again we are being separated from the general current of literature, situated in a place where only women are allowed to enter, a small and isolated place where we will be protected but segregated. When we finally believed, after so many generations, that we had gained the freedom to wander all over the house, once again we are all sent packing to the kitchen, to the laundry room, to some place for women only. As writers, we would like to compete on the same playing field as our male colleagues. Instead, we are relegated to special lanes where only women can run, where we won't disturb or occupy the space designated for men. We suspect that in those lanes the demands for quality are fewer and that what is feminine is considered as some type of handicap. We fear, above all, that the subject of literature written by women, closes off our access to the criticism that addresses the specific literary value of our texts. For many years in Latin America, the demand for social "commitment" interfered with the aesthetic consideration of the works themselves. We would not want a political definition of what is considered feminine to produce that same effect.

Separation by gender is an antiquated, machista aspiration present in almost all short story collections and literary criticism in Latin American countries. In general, women are not present in anthologies in adequate proportions (except as token women authors). The panorama is completed and guilt is eased by preparing anthologies just for women (that in general are not read by male readers). Since we are also rarely mentioned in articles and other works of literary criticism that present a history of Latin American literature, these omissions are compensated for by including separate chapters dedicated to "women who write." These chapters group together writers from very different eras and with different tendencies with no justification other than their gender.

However, that mistrust is reduced when we see that currently there is a genuine interest in the United States in becoming familiar with and studying the writing by women of Latin America. Our writing has become an integral part of the programs of study in many universities, and researchers are extremely careful to proceed in a politically-correct manner.

Within this new context, when we consider that many of these researchers, as well as the general reading public, have no other means of access to the writing by Latin American women, this type of collection begins to be justified. That is if the selection, as in the case of *Cruel Fictions, Cruel Realities*, has been chosen for its aesthetic and literary value, rather than for ideological reasons.

Literature and militancy: A double-edged sword

All throughout history, women writers have suffered different types of preconceived impositions with respect to what and how they should write. The most overtly misogynist position simply excluded women from writing literature: this position banished those women with a literary vocation to the periphery, where they then focused on the genres of correspondence and the intimate diary. Later, different types of "permissions" began to surface allowing women writers to publish.

Today, a very different problem exists, that nonetheless provokes the former effects. Feminist criticism and feminine collections can function like a double-edged sword, attempting to unify literature written by women, but at the same time ignoring the diversity in their eagerness to find common threads. This new danger, which tends to ignore differences or eradicate them, appears in feminist criticism, often ignoring the intrinsic literary value of the works. As with any work of ideological criticism, as happened in the 1960s with certain Marxist criticism, feminist criticism is interested in verifying whether certain political models are completed. It attempts to establish if a particular work is positive or negative regarding the social condition of women: women should only write about other women; their protagonists should be strong and brave, but constrained by the social medium; their female protagonists should always be good, happy, generous, and unjustly overpowered or attacked. This criticism is valid, useful, and defensible for feminism, but it doesn't serve literature very well, and it begins to become truly menacing when it tries to impose a doctrine all women writers should abide by in order to be real women.

What we call "Latin America"

Taking for granted that Latin America exists is almost an exaggeration. When a Latin American writer presents him/herself to a foreign public, they utter their first words, with the intention of highlighting their differences. "Don't think that my country…" "Don't think that my country is a combination of mangoes, the tropics, Borges, baroque, and Patagonia, where we are usually confused by those from the Other World." We writers rebel when the Other World looks at us. We rebel at that outside scrutiny which places so many cultural, dialectal, rhythmical, and stylistic differences in the same bag. We sometimes rebel to the point of denying that which is evident: language and history, our history of similar, parallel, and interconnected misfortunes. Which Latin America are we talking about? The Caribbean? The Incan? The one with the samba? The one with the cueca? The Patagonian? The Aztecan? The Latin America that constantly asks, time and time again, about its identity without receiving an appropriate or definitive response?

Today, many of us writers who live in the great cities of Latin America perceive, with a certain horror, that the critics, the readers, and the publishing houses are attempting to push us toward a permanent exhibition of supposedly typical values. It's not enough to have been born in Latin America, not enough to live there; we have to also constantly exhibit it in our work in order to awaken the interest of the public as well as the publishers. Our words should smell like guavas, like the jungle, or at least like the vast pampas, even though our reality consists of concrete and video games.

In this sense, Professor Leonard's collection saves us from this prejudice. These stories, which are so varied, in no way attempt to define any type of "local color" nor to provide a "typical" profile of a Latin America, which, in many cases, only exists in the pitiful fantasy of a certain "First World."

The thematic axis: Its dual function
The majority of these stories show some type of relation to the theme of cruelty. This choice is quite interesting to me, precisely because it serves to demythify two versions of femininity, that from the past to the present, have attempted to limit women's writing.

Dating from Romanticism, Courtly Love and the Middle Ages, the notion that women are tender and velvet-covered still exists, as does the idea that they are incapable not only of committing evil deeds, but of even imagining them. Women, who were thought to be naturally gifted for love and nurturing (and nothing else), were only capable of giving caresses or of imagining them. As silly as this supposition might be, it has for centuries limited the participation of women in all the arts, where cruelty and death are essential elements in the reality of all women. In order to adapt to this idealized vision of themselves, women who could have been talented painters have limited themselves for centuries to painting watercolor flowers: an equivalent limitation also influenced the production of literature.

Presently, the danger in limitation lies in what is considered to be politically-correct in feminine literature, and which *Cruel Fictions, Cruel Realities* firmly dismisses. Here, there are no protagonists with forced kindness, no protagonists who are generous or full of that mysterious earthly wisdom that is so unjustly said to be an essential quality of Latin American women. Here, there are only human beings in all their terrible contradictions, in their ignorance, their doubt, and in their distressed humanity.

This is precisely the common thematic axis which demonstrates the absolute variety feminine writing can adopt. Professor Leonard has defined herself through freedom. Her writers face cruelty through all possible genres (fantasy, terror, realism, and naturalism), and through all imaginable protagonists (women, children, men, and the elderly).

A selection of stories without prejudices

I must admit that when I first glanced at the list of stories and writers, I felt disconcerted. The majority of the authors were unknown to me, which in itself is not so surprising when dealing with writers from other countries, since cultural communication ties among Latin American countries are tenuous. Currently, authors from Latin America must be published in Madrid in order for their books to circulate on their own continent. But nonetheless, here we do not see the great names of the contemporary bestselling authors we all know, and I can boast about being familiar with the literature written by women in my own country, Argentina. Still, included here in this collection is an Argentine author with whom I am not familiar.

With certain reticence, then, I began to read these stories, and their literary quality confronted me with my own prejudices. These authors, many of whom are unknown outside of their limited zones, are excellent writers who deserve to be read.

The fact that this anthology does not include many of the most well-known names of Latin American literature is one more merit of the editor, who, at the risk of creating a book which is less saleable, makes available material that would otherwise be very difficult to obtain even for those who study this topic. Professor Leonard must be lauded for not resorting once again to the recourse of publishing the same time-honored authors as always whose writings are easily accessible to most of us anyway.

What these authors do and do not have in common

Contemporary Latin American authors are intensely different from each other, and it's important to us that these differences be considered and appreciated. We are not interested in being forcibly united from a political stance.

However, I should also admit all that we do have in common. We have language in common; it differs in its multitude of dialect variations, but remains Spanish nonetheless. We have geography in common, enormously varied, but which ultimately gathers us all within the same continent. It is geography that forces us to share the same neighbors and that so quickly transforms itself into geopolitics, into history. We have in common a history, shared to such a degree that when a democratic government materializes in Latin America, others follow it like a row of dominoes.

Above all, we Latin American authors have in common an enormous need for the dissemination of our work. Anthologies such as this one are crucial if our work is to become known outside of our individual countries. Professor Leonard has succeeded in appreciating and exhibiting the infinite possibilities of writing in all its diversity. These stories differ in thematic content, in writing style, in their approximation of reality, in their ideology, in the structure of the texts, and in their focus on feminine identity, sexuality, and the world. Welcome, *Cruel Fictions, Cruel Realities.*

Translated by Kathy S. Leonard

Introduction

This anthology resulted from a personal need to compile a collection of short stories by relatively unknown Latin American women writers—an anthology that would be suitable for use in university courses dealing with Hispanic literature in translation. I believed that such a collection would also be useful to other university instructors, who often make use of the short story in courses dealing with women's studies, social and political sciences, and Latin American history, since short stories often very accurately portray the culture, customs, and sociopolitical situations of the people of Latin America. I am confident that this anthology will fill such a need, and that, additionally, it will be of interest to many other readers outside of the classroom who wish to expand their knowledge of foreign literatures and cultures.

The past several decades have seen an enormous literary production by Latin American writers, men as well as women, creating a new awareness and appreciation for Latin American literature in readers in the United States. A recent "boom" of sorts has been triggered by a new generation of writers who are becoming more widely known as their works are translated into English and other languages. Greater interest and visibility have led to an increase in the publication of anthologies that contain work by Latin American authors, and it is particularly gratifying to see that many of these anthologies are dedicated to publishing the work of women writers. I cite as examples several of the more recent anthologies dealing exclusively with fiction by women writers: *What is Secret: Stories by Chilean Women* (1995), *Daughters of the Fifth Sun: A Collection of Latina Fiction and Poetry* (1995), *In Other Words: Literature by Latinas of the United States* (1994), *Pleasure in the Word: Erotic Writing by Latin American Women* (1994), *Compañeras: Latina Lesbians (An Anthology)* (1994), *Landscapes of a New Land: Short Fiction by Latin American Women* (1993), *Secret Weavers: Stories of the Fantastic by Women of Argentina and Chile* (1993), and *One Hundred Years After Tomorrow: Brazilian Women's Fiction in the 20th Century* (1992). [1]

Although many publications of women's work currently exist, critical attention has focused on a relatively small group of writers. Names such as Isabel Allende, Luisa Valenzuela, Rosario Castellanos,

Clarice Lispector, and Rosario Ferré, among others, are familiar to many readers, even to those who do not have extensive knowledge of Latin American literature. Wishing to offset this trend in some way, my intention with the publication of *Cruel Fictions, Cruel Realities* was not to simply add one more anthology to the many that include the authors most of us are familiar with, but rather to create a unique volume of work by "new" authors who are excellent writers but who have not yet established a reputation or who have simply been overlooked by editors and translators. The time is right to introduce new faces into the arena, to hear new voices that deserve increased exposure and that can make significant contributions to Latin American women's literature.

Very few readers will be familiar with the majority of the writers included here, even those readers well-acquainted with writing by women writers from Latin American. Although many of the writers have won national and international writing awards, their work has not been widely disseminated outside of their native countries. I offer as an example Yolanda Bedregal, who is considered to be one of Bolivia's most important writers, yet who is little known outside of her own country. Only a few of her short stories have been translated into English or included in anthologies published in English-speaking countries. Ana María Shua, who has published over fifteen books (several of them considered best sellers) in her native Argentina since 1967, is only now beginning to receive recognition in the United States. Many of her stories have been translated and included in anthologies and in literary journals, and several of her novels are currently being translated into English.

The majority of the authors included in this anthology have never before had their work translated, and most likely would have little or no dissemination of their stories outside of their native countries if not for anthologies which strive to include lesser-known authors. Several of the stories included here, specifically "The Visit" and "The Vigil" by Nayla Chehade Durán, and "The Hunchback," by Mirta Toledo, have not been published previously.

I purposely sought out work by living authors so I would benefit from their input and collaboration on the translations, biographies, and bibliographies. This strategy proved to be quite successful, as well as essential. Little or no published information is available about these writers in the United States. Ultimately it needed to be provided by the authors themselves. As for the translations, I chose to undertake all of them myself. This resulted in an enjoyable and enriching experience, which was also quite challenging at times. Some of the translations proceeded easily with few difficulties; others, however, did not, and were hindered due to problematic linguistic constructions as well as my unfamiliarity with certain cultural elements. The stories by Nayla Chehade Durán were by far the most difficult. The lyrical quality of "The Vigil" is one of the elements which makes the story so alluring, but it is also the very element which made it so difficult to translate. Concerning the art of translation, Alexis Levitin comments: "Translators are condemned to fail, because sound and sense, form and content, are so intimately meshed in serious writing, the translator can only hope for a noble effort, an honorable defeat. Translation must be imperfect." [2] When confronted with the poetic language in "The Vigil," I made my most noble effort, and then sought out the author for advice and suggestions. The resulting translation is the product of a collaboration and does not fully replicate the beauty of the original, but it does approximate it as nearly as our combined abilities allowed. Chehade Durán's second story, "The Visit," presented further stylistic challenges. Any translator who works with Spanish and English is well aware of the differences in syntactic constructions and punctuation use between the two languages. In the case of "The Visit," the author wished to maintain her original punctuation and sentence and paragraph length, although these elements did not always mesh with English usage. Whenever possible in the translations, I have respected the wishes and suggestions of authors, insisting on certain usage only when comprehension or readability might have been compromised.

Other than my desire to locate well-written, interesting, and thought-provoking work for this anthology, no particular theme guided my search for stories in the initial stages. As is the case with many anthologies, the work contained in them reflects the personal tastes of the editor, and this is partially true for this anthology as well. I selected stories that I liked, but I also attempted to choose stories from a variety of countries as well as stories that represent a broad spectrum of literary techniques, styles, and thematic content. I asked friends, colleagues, and students to read my selections and offer their opinions. Many of them commented on the grim and dark nature of the stories, advising me to balance the anthology by including stories which were less depressing. After giving this suggestion a good deal of thought, I rejected it, instead utilizing their well-meant observation as a basis for identifying the theme of cruelty which unifies these stories.

One may well question the choice of a theme such as cruelty, but I feel it is a very important as well as a valid criterion on which to base a collection of short stories. Many readers have the misconception that women authors write stories only about women and treat subjects that are of importance to women only. This is not true, and the reading of work by Latin American women writers will quickly reveal that women are no less concerned than male writers with the articulation and denouncement of poverty, corruption and the abuse of power, clashes between differing sociocultural elements, friction between traditional and modern values in a changing society, as well as other negative forces currently destroying their countries. At the same time, women authors seem to be more sensitive and intimate in their treatment of subjects such as love, death, other human relationships, and the struggles to rise above traditional limitations responsible for women's underdevelopment and oppression. If one wishes to find a common theme in women's writing in the Third World, it might be that these writers share a vision of hope for the future development of their own country and for all of Latin America.

Considering Latin America's violent history, replete with wide-spread violence, numerous dictatorships, bloody civil wars, kidnappings, thousands of disappeared persons, torture, human rights abuses, and the oppression of women, children, and other marginalized groups, it should not be surprising that Latin American authors should choose to "document" these events in their writing. These writers are often the ones who figure most prominently among those who are committed to political and social change, with women many times being among the most outspoken. The Bolivian critic Hugo Lijeron Alberdi concurs, believing that some of the most violent literature currently appearing is being written by women in Latin America. [3] Women are quick to voice their dissatisfaction and frustration through their work, questioning the established norms by exposing the harsh realities of contemporary Latin America. David William Foster, in his book titled *Violence in Argentine Literature*, feels that this trend is due to the fact that many Latin American writers, men as well as women, consider themselves to be the spokespersons for society, taking it upon themselves to write against social and political oppression. According to Foster, their writing "gives voice to individuals, groups, or sets of experiences that might not otherwise be heard." [4]

The fact that women can literarily imagine, describe, and enjoy cruelty, violence, and horror is widely demonstrated in all forms in this anthology. The stories collected here offer unique portrayals of human experiences, allowing the reader to view the many faces of cruelty presented from a woman's perspective. However, these are not stories about cruelty, torture, or abuse of women, but stories about the cruelty perpetrated by one human being on another or by a government on its citizens, a cruelty which is multifaceted and omnipresent. These writers expose the hidden and overt dangers of cruelty, showing us that cruelty emerges from many sources, expected as well as unexpected, from sources known and unknown, and has the ability to embolden its perpetrators with a thirst for increased power that allows them to perpetuate their cycle of terror and abuse.

Several of the stories deal with the pervasive political instability so common in many Latin American countries, which can have a profound and often fatal effect on innocent citizens. In Velia Calvimontes' story, "Coati 1950," a young boy who has committed a minor infraction struggles to survive in a prison labor camp where the guards entertain themselves by inflicting physical and mental torture on their captives. In "The Morgue," Yolanda Bedregal describes a country under siege (Bolivia's revolution of 1952) where life is meaningless and death is the ultimate equalizer. Social class and economic status are irrelevant to the pile of corpses stacked in a hospital corridor, which are robbed and violated by the living, whose only motive in doing so is survival. In "The Vigil," Chehade Durán details the poverty and misery of a town forgotten by its own government, a town whose moral and physical disintegration mirrors that of its dictator.

More often than not, the cruelty depicted in these stories is subtle and insidious. It is the day-to-day cruelty family members inflict upon one another, such as parents' rejection of their son's choice of bride due to her physical characteristics in Silvia Diez Fierro's "The Sailor's Wife." Or it is the cruelty of parents to their daughter in Gloria Artigas's "Corners of Smoke," where apathy and neglect not only damage the child's psyche but also cause her to be diminished, literally and figuratively. It is the remnants of cruelty lodged in a child's memory in Yolanda Bedregal's "How Milinco Escaped from School," where the most positive comment a boy makes about his dead father is that he didn't beat him too frequently. Sometimes children are as equally skilled as their parents in participating in cruel and inhumane acts. Viviana Mellet's "Good Night Air" portrays a guilt-ridden adult son who fantasizes about the death of his ailing mother, whose absence, he believes, will ultimately save his marriage. In desperation, he performs a simple act of "humane cruelty," an act that he hopes will cause his fantasy to materialize. Very young children, although perhaps unaware of the magnitude of their actions, are also capable of committing acts of cruelty. In Inés Fernández Moreno's "A Mother to Be Assembled," the children are oblivious to the repercussions of their behavior, and make repeated selfish and disfiguring demands on their mother, who selflessly complies with these requests out of a sense of duty and a misguided notion of how a "good mother" should behave.

Cruelty is also a common element found in situations where one human being wields power over another. Ana María Shua, using a graphic sense of black humor in "A Profession Like Any Other," allows a sadistic dentist to take revenge on an unsuspecting patient whose only crime is being related to a former deadbeat patient of the dentist. Shua's story highlights the use of medical science as an instrument of terror and abuse, not so unlike the terror felt by citizens in Argentina during the rule of military dictatorships. Similarly, a classroom becomes an environment ripe for the abuse of position and power in Gilda Holst Molestina's "The Competition," in which a teacher cruelly and gleefully ridicules and manipulates the adolescent insecurities and fears of his young students, only to himself suffer from well-aimed revenge on the part of those he so callously tortured.

As grim as some of the stories may be, they offer, often with touches of humor, and sometimes with brutal frankness, a particular perspective on life in Latin America. While authors may fictionalize events specific to their individual countries through the use of local details and other identifying occurrences, these stories are also universal, for they express the hopes and desires of a collective people, their triumphs and disappointments, their lives and deaths. These stories contain neither heroes nor heroines, but, rather, simple human beings who are overwhelmed and exhausted by their circumstances. Despite the bleakness of their landscapes, the writers of these stories refuse to be overcome by the violence, cruelty, and apparent hopelessness of their societies. With their words they are sowing seeds, confident that these seeds will germinate in the minds of their readers, eventually bearing fruit in the collective consciousness of a global society.

Kathy S. Leonard
Iowa State University, Ames

Notes to the introduction

1. For a complete, annotated list of anthologies containing Latin American women's work in translation, see Kathy S. Leonard's *Index to Translated Short Fiction by Latin American Women in English Language Anthologies*, forthcoming from Greenwood Press.

2. For further insights into Levitin's philosophy of translation, see *Soulstorm: Stories by Clarice Lispector* (New York: A New Directions book, 1976) 171.

3. Hugo Lijeron Alberdi, *Los Premios (Estudio de las novelas ganadoras del Premio de Novela "Erich Guttentag" 1969-1986).* (La Paz: Editorial Los Amigos del Libro, 1987) 152.

4. David William Foster, *Violence in Argentine Literature: Cultural Responses to Tyranny.* (Columbia and London: University of Missouri Press, 1995) 46.

Gloria Artigas is a retired professor from the Universidad Técnica del Estado in Santiago, Chile, where she worked for twenty-five years in the language department. Although she had written numerous works in Spanish as well as in English, she did not seriously dedicate herself to the writing of fiction until after she retired in 1980. Shortly thereafter, she moved to the seaside resort of Santo Domingo on the central coast of Chile, and it was there that she began to write her first stories.

Artigas feels that there have been two important influences in her literary production: her professional preparation as an educator and her passionate interest in literature, initiated at a very young age when she read many classical writers from Spain, England, and the United States. However, once she moved to Santo Domingo, she was initially motivated in her writing by the people she encountered in the Port of San Antonio, very near her home. Her increasing familiarity with the fishermen and their families, with the laborers, and the artists and crafts people of the region, gave her an appreciation of the strength these people possessed when constantly confronted with the unpredictability of nature, such as frequent earthquakes and floods. She was also inspired by the energy of the women of the area, who, in spite of their impoverished circumstances, still strove to support their families and to progress.

Artigas says that her story "Corners of Smoke" surfaced spontaneously as she struggled with an idea concerning the lack of communication among human beings. In this story we encounter the cruelty of family members toward one another, a cruelty which does not stem from physical trauma or even from verbal abuse, but from simple neglect, which ultimately is more devastating in its effect than many other types of abuse.

Gloria Artigas has won several awards for her writing, and "Corners of Smoke" was named as first honorable mention in the Second Latin American Competition of the Short Story Written by Women in 1993.

Corners of Smoke

by Gloria Artigas

I often thought about my family's house, and each time I did, a certain chilling sensation ran through my body and a feeling of loneliness remained. The house was an enormous structure of rooms brimming with old and twisted furniture; its massiveness gave it the appearance of a museum full of abandoned rooms. It had useless spaces jammed with objects no one ever used and an infinite number of corridors that came out of nowhere and led to closed doors. It was a very large and strange house, perhaps with a perverse personality, because it seemed to reject even the light that came through its tiny windows covered by lace curtains. The walls were lined with portraits of unknown people.

We used to live there, my parents and I. I use the expression "used to live" because it is the most common way to phrase it, but it might be better to say: we tolerated each other's existence. My mother was an old woman then, indifferent to anything that wasn't her wish or need. In her youth she had been a happy woman with a sparkling and contagious sense of humor. Everything revolved around her in that house: it seemed natural and unquestionable to us. In time her face took on a tense expression and her lips showed a rictus of permanent disapproval. However, she maintained her sense of observation which became increasingly sharper and more penetrating. It reached the point where, when submitting to her interrogations, I felt as if my body were transparent, like an x ray, where it was impossible to hide its interior under her strong and hypnotic stare.

We dragged around our silent existence. I constantly paraded through the house with a book in my hands and no desire to read. My parents prolonged their dialogues of absolute silence day after day in card games that allowed them to exist without communicating with one another. Many times they insisted that I also participate; I would obstinately refuse, perhaps it was the only one of their demands that I could refuse…I thought that if I became involved in the diabolical entertainment that caused the players to lose their voices and live through the cards, I would end up like the queens drawn by their hands: stiff and colorful, without a life of their own.

Once I met a young boy who became a friend. He was a clerk in a store where I bought things the few times I went out, since the shopping was done by one of my aunts who came by several times a week. For the first time I knew what it was like to smile, and after talking with the boy a few times, I dared to invite him to my house. As soon as he arrived, an electric current could be felt in the air. My father took advantage of the suspension of the card game to go and smoke his cigarettes in one of the numerous corners of the house.

My mother changed the permanent expression on her face and greeted the new arrival with a coquettish smile, surely rescued for the occasion from a pale memory of her past when she was a beautiful and attractive woman.

"How nice it is to know that our daughter has friends because she's a very strange girl and never talks to anyone!"

"That's curious, because I don't have that impression, Señora; my name is Darío and I would like to go out with your daughter."

"I don't think that will be a problem, but first I must consult with my husband. We are very old fashioned."

My mother and Darío then became absorbed in a conversation filled with nonsense, not even allowing me to open my mouth. After awhile, my mother politely said good-bye to Darío, sure she would never see him again. And so it was.

The time passed slowly. I noticed that my father began to diminish in size. Everyday he looked smaller and everyday a greater quantity of smoke floated from the corners in the house. The card games were interrupted more and more frequently: I sensed a silent struggle between two personalities that refused to be trapped by each other.

My father, now so tiny that he could fit in the dresser drawer, died suddenly. That was the first time I had seen anyone die, and his allowing himself to go with no resistance and without searching for support had a profound effect on me. He closed his eyes and a spark came out of his mouth: a luminous thread that bounced off the ceiling and broke into tiny lights. I remained there, seated at his side, watching him, hypnotized as I contemplated a tranquility so complete, something I longed to enjoy in life.

Soon after that, I began to climb up to the small attic. It became my only home, a place that was truly mine. I would situate myself in front of the window where I could look outside, and during those moments, I felt alive. I would experience something strange: I would confuse myself with the people dressed in colorful clothing who passed by all day long on the street below. I would imagine that I was inside a kaleidoscope, and when it turned, I was a minute and colorful part of a brilliant world that didn't stop, but which constantly changed shapes and hues. "Is that how life is?" a small voice would ask, always anxiously interrupting my amusement.

Other times from my observation point I would see women with their small children pass by. Then I would hurry to the rocking chair and take my beautiful baby doll in my arms. I would communicate to him the warmth and love I had always longed for and he was always waiting for. During those moments it was evident that this was my life, and that what occurred in the rest of it was only an image, dream, or nightmare.

My mother began to grow alarmingly in size. She looked taller and thicker, she rarely spoke: she only gave orders with a look. My aunt came to live with us and took my father's place in the frenetic card games. The routine did not change.

Only now it was I who hid in the corners to smoke the cigarettes I found in my father's drawers. My mother and aunt would look around in anguish, trying to discover where the smoke was coming from; they believed, with all certainty, that it was the final rebellion of the diminutive old man who had departed, leaving spirals of smoke floating through the corridors.

Some strange evil had attacked my mother as she grew more immense and could no longer fit in the double bed. I noticed her absence one day; no one explained anything to me and I didn't attempt to find out. That's how it should have been and I accepted it. I felt pain mixed with relief. Pain because I didn't know how she disappeared: perhaps she left through one of the corridors and opened the wrong door. My relief came from feeling free for the first time from those scrutinizing looks that had kept me from being myself.

I stayed with my aunt, a sweet and sad being, as if that sadness, poorly inherited, had adhered to the skin of everyone in the family. The poor old woman tried to talk with me, but I had lost the habit, and I was beginning to stop thinking too, which made me feel happy inside. I had no one to tell me things secretly, because that tiny inquisitive voice inside me had also been extinguished.

When I went up to the attic, I noticed that I was also shrinking in size. This confirmation was terrifying for me: I could hardly climb the steps that led to my real life.

I no longer go down the stairs now. I am reclining in an armchair next to my rubber doll: we are nearly the same size now and at last I have found total peace. I no longer think, but I believe that I have never moved from this chair where there were always two rubber dolls.

My aunts who stayed to live on the floor below have lost all hope of selling the house: spirals of smoke drift from every corner, and the creaking of something immense can be heard passing through all the rooms, ever vigilant.

Yolanda Bedregal is a poet, novelist, short story writer, and sculptor. She was born into an artistic and intellectual family in La Paz, Bolivia in 1916, and her parents, Juan Francisco Bedregal and Carmen Iturri, greatly influenced the path her life would take. She studied fine arts at the Universidad de San Andrés, later becoming a professor at the same university, teaching courses in aesthetics and art history. In 1936, she traveled to the United States as the first Bolivian woman to receive a scholarship to study at Barnard College.

Bedregal has worked and taught in various regions of Bolivia: at the Escuela Superior de Bellas Artes, at the Conservatorio de Música, and at the Academia Benavides. She has worked tirelessly to promote the dissemination of literature in her country by founding the National Union of Poets and the Committee on Children's Literature.

Bedregal is considered one of Bolivia's most important authors, and in her long literary career, she has published over sixteen books. Other publications include over fifty articles dealing with the history of art for children, articles on pedagogy, religion, myth, folklore, and Aymara and Quechua folk art. Many of her poems have been translated into various languages and included in journals and anthologies in the United States and Europe.

Bedregal has received numerous awards for her writing, among them, the Premio Nacional de Poesía, the Premio Nacional del Ministerio de Cultura, Honor al Mérito, the Premio Nacional de Novela "Erich Guttentag" for her novel *Bajo el oscuro sol*, and most recently the Condecoración Franz Tamayo en el grado de Gran Cruz, awarded by the Prefectura del Departamento de La Paz, Bolivia, in 1995.

Bedregal's story, "How Milinco Escaped from School," shows her sympathy for and understanding of adolescents. "I can imagine what might happen to a young boy who joins the circus. The circus is something that appears repeatedly in my work, because, as I have often said in my 'confessions,' I would have liked to belong to a circus, and when I was young, I even walked on an imaginary tight rope, which was really nothing more than a board in the wooden floor of our house."

"The Morgue" is an excerpt from Bedregal's award-winning novel *Bajo el oscuro sol*, which deals with the life of a young woman who is killed by a stray bullet while writing in her room. The woman's writings are subsequently discovered by her former professor, and the story unfolds as a novel within a novel, allowing the reader insights into Bedregal's early feminist tendencies. The chapter "The Morgue," foreshadows the young woman's death and details the horrors of a country in the throes of a revolution.

Yolanda Bedregal currently lives in La Paz, Bolivia, with her daughter Rosángela, and continues to be active in literary organizations.

How Milinco Escaped from School

by Yolanda Bedregal

Milinco, with his soul feeling restless within his body, wasn't learning his lessons. But his sweet shyness and his gray eyes communicated great tranquility. The teacher, upset by the mischievousness of the other children, used to look at Milinco like one searching for some measure of comfort. Ah, if only all the children could have the same expression as that little face, the atmosphere at school would be very different.

That Monday, the teacher felt abandoned. Why had Milinco missed class? He didn't usually play hooky; he was never sick.

Milinco had left his house early for school. The morning, just like the boy, looked as if it had been recently washed. The air was pleasant and cold, the sky blue. It seemed as if at any moment the houses would take off, disrupting the rows they formed while climbing up to the mountains.

Milinco lost his way and walked away from the city with the sensation that everything was following his steps, the trees, sidewalks, buildings. And the higher he climbed, the more things seemed to be at his feet, so obedient was the world in his freedom and in his pure joy of walking. It hurt him to see girls walking to school with wet hair, wearing their white smocks, stiff from the creases of the iron, not yet settled on their bodies. Poor girls! Why were they going to school when everything outside sang of freedom? He would have liked to stop them on this windy winter day on the plateau and ask: "Why are you going to school, María?" But he called without moving his lips. He continued walking and walking.

Suddenly he found himself in front of several canvas tents that looked like the sails of a ship in repose. He jumped a fence and reached the camp, creeping along until he arrived at the main tent. A gramophone cranked out a barcarole by Hoffman. He crossed the sawdust road to the arena, which was surrounded by a framework of boards making up the bleachers. The chairs were in disarray; candy wrappers were on the ground, crumpled programs and photographs rested on the chairs.

Milinco inhaled the air of the recently abandoned enclosure.

At school, he would pass through the empty spaces created by his classmates after they left. There were remnants from the more persistent students, from others, the signs were barely perceptible, and from some, not even a trace remained. Milinco recognized the children by the intensity of the absence they left when they fled the classroom, by the attitude of the desks as they awaited their owners. Anxious places, rejected and indifferent.

Here, in an empty circus, that sensation, which had always fascinated him, was much more exciting; even the air trapped inside the canvas was like that of a transient guest. Traces of momentary laughter and impersonal sadness hung in the air.

The barcarole stopped, and immediately, a man wearing a braided jacket appeared, carrying the gramophone into the arena. He placed it in a corner and began to wind it. The apparatus screeched and squawked disagreeably, reluctant to work as a substitute for the orchestra, until the man forced it into action by placing the sharp needle on the record. With the first notes, a little girl dressed as a ragged butterfly, who looked as if she had escaped from a bramble patch, emerged in little hops. The trainer fastened her by her knotted hair to a hook which hung from a cable; he gave her a small plate to bite, and he began to raise her off the ground. Her little arms crossed over her chest, her tiny body arched backwards, and she balanced herself in a spiral of ever-increasing speed. She continued the spins on the pulley—it dropped or stretched, obedient to the wishes of the trainer. If she made an error, the whip cracked, and there was a dull moan from the injured butterfly, like a funeral flower, until the move was executed correctly.

Then the galloping of a white pony burst into the arena. The trick rider, dressed in a blue skirt and tights, mounted the horse in one jump. She slid agilely onto the platform on the horse's back, then to the hind quarters, as if she were walking on the crest of a wave. The instructor's authoritative voice was raising an expectant dust of torture between the animal's head and the tulle of the rider's short skirt.

The rehearsal of other acts followed. The man of steel, who at one time had been able to lift heavy weights during the show with a smile, now writhed in agony, painfully sweating from the effort, with swollen veins and a reddened face. Could Milinco ever enjoy the circus again? Perhaps it would be better to return to the city which awaited him.

Instead of leaving the tent, his unrelenting subconscious forced him to search out the manager.

"Mister, can I join the circus?"

"What do you know how to do? We have enough loafers already that I'd gladly be rid of. No way, kid, no!"

Embarrassed, Milinco began to leave. Something whispered in the manager's ear, causing him to think twice. "Listen, listen, kid! You, with the little flag on your back. Come here, you little ragamuffin. I'm going to take you on! But you have to behave yourself, okay? You'll feed the animals, and that's it! You'll get food and a bed, and that's all I'm responsible for. There must be a job for a boy of your age. How old are you?"

"Fifteen."

"I would have guessed twelve, but you're sickly. You can stay. But first tell me, do you have parents? Where do you live?"

Milinco again betrayed himself; "I'm an orphan. I live on the street with the shoe-shine boys."

"Fine, fine, but I warn you, you can't leave here today; tonight is the last show, and tomorrow we pack up the tents. Day after tomorrow we leave. You understand?"

Milinco didn't usually lie, nor did he think he was lying now by saying "I'm an orphan." It was true that his father had died; his heart had killed him. He hadn't been a bad father, the boy admitted to himself, he had rarely hit him.

But based on those three murderous words, he invented his truth and built upon it during that night of his first insomnia.

"I'm an orphan!" And he began to work as the animals' guardian, animals that had been plucked from their natural environment for the enjoyment of the people in the city.

Milinco did not object to them changing his name. He was no longer the boy who had skipped school to obey the morning's call. He was a magnificent shepherd who had brought his urban countryside along with him, to follow him all over the world like an errant flock, forever under the awnings inflated and deflated by the wind on each day's journey.

Every time the tents were raised in a town, his lungs filled with a new song. And every time the canvas folded its white bat-like wings and the chairs were dismantled, he felt his fantasy ship become anchored. It was absence and presence, song and echo, which he had so longed for in his infancy without knowing it. Leaving and arriving, having and losing, beginning and ending, day and night, the continuous swell of existence on the open ocean of his own life.

On the empty bench at school, the teacher searched in vain for consolation in those gray eyes now contemplating the barley dancing between the thick lips of the circus animals.

The Morgue

(Excerpt from *Bajo el oscuro sol*)

by Yolanda Bedregal

*T*he sick day gasped for breath. It was six o'clock. Near the Plaza Venezuela, students and workers had uprooted tiles, benches, light posts, and they were forming barricades. Loreto couldn't return to her boarding house. Her hunger, nerves, and fear, caused her to see everything as if it were floating.

She spotted a food vendor on a corner and moved toward her, forgetting about the danger. Purple stew boiled in a large kettle over a fire, and the woman ladled a thick stream of it into a steaming cup which she then extended to the young woman. Loreto gulped down the velvet liquid with pleasure. The vision of her house now seemed far away.

Loreto had barely swallowed the last gulp when, not knowing how, she found herself buried in an avalanche of soldiers. Carried along by their shoving and kicking, she was forced onto the back of a truck that was being used to transport the dead. Loreto crouched down among some tarps, avoiding brushing against the row of oscillating feet that pointed to the sky, some barefoot, others wearing sandals, army boots, moccasins, or nothing but socks.

Only extremities—the faces were covered by rolled-up jackets.

The truck stopped at various places. The dead could wait. The living joked about the inheritance of their "clients." On the way to

Miraflores, the truck's shadow stretched and contracted. Sharp-sounding detonations crucified the city. The vehicle threaded its way down the Avenida del Ejército. When it was almost to the bridge, the Choqueyapu launched a reproach with a thick stream of smoke. Several soldiers lost their balance and fell to their knees among the cadavers. Only one recruit turned pale; the others laughed. The hospital gate squeaked slightly as it was opened by the guards. White smocks and nuns' habits flapped hurriedly through the hallways. Instruments clanked on rolling tables. Behind the hospital there was a poorly-paved area where the morgue was located, next to a colonial style church.

As the truck passed, desperate people climbed up onto the open bed. Loreto took advantage of the confusion to escape her hiding place and lose herself among the workers who were unloading the cadavers using a board as a slide.

To the right of the atrium, some thirty bodies lay scattered on the ground like fish on a dock. Stepping on them, separating them, men and women from every walk of life pushed one another in their frenzy to recognize their relatives. Crying, yelling, sobbing, desolate whispering. An Indian couple talked of their despair in Spanish with Aymara syntax. "In vain all the faces I have looked at. No Silvicu is there. Always he is not there. The great God does not permit it. I am sure that he was with those *wainas* with their brains coming out like they are; that red wool cap and pouch; of course, that's them. The shoes we will notice. Those for his birthday which we gave him, he put on. Of course he must be here; wearing those shoes with their yellow toes and white laces, he is."

A boy, witness to the peasants' grief, slipped off to one side and whispered to his companion:

"Pass the shoes to Mokho, so he can sneak off. They're the owners of that dead man." And he nodded toward them with a professional wink. The small thief hid the shoes under his jacket and slithered away among the mourners.

Loreto felt the urge to grab the youngster by the scruff of his neck and report him in a loud voice. But it was already useless. Their coordinated effort had been too quick.

The peasants wouldn't find their son; his face had been destroyed and the articles of clothing they would have used to identify him were in the hands of a thief.

Anger and impotence were added to their pain.

A car bearing official plates stopped at the service door. The occupants got out; they ordered the lieutenant to open the dissection room. They entered, elbowing aside those who attempted to slip through. When the partition was half-opened, one could glimpse, not faces, but military and civilian apparel, and could smell the odor of filth and disinfectant.

"Don't open for anyone, do you understand?"

"At your service, jefe."

In the meantime, the shadows of the survivors stretched at length over the dead. The hospital alarm sounded simultaneously in all sections. A doctor advanced toward the morgue and summoned the people together: "Listen, please! Can I have your attention?" Successively in Spanish, Ayamara, and Quechua, in a firm and paternal voice, he addressed the group.

"I am the director of the hospital. I share in your sorrow. At this very moment, the injured are being attended to in the operating room. Some have already been sent home. Those who have fallen are here. They are heroes who honor our country, and you should be proud of these valiant men and women. One day we will have a better Bolivia thanks to them."

"That's a lie, Doctor, a lie. They're not heroes and they're not valiant," an angry, sobbing voice interrupted. "They're killing them. We don't even know why we shout 'long live Bolivia' because they're killing our people...My son was carrying water to the injured..."

"Be calm, Señora, I beg of you. Don't torment yourself. We're all suffering. Listen to me, we have to close the gate. Tomorrow you can come and collect your dead. Meanwhile, the priest and nuns will watch over them tonight and pray."

"We also know how to pray! We're not leaving this place even if you whip us," an energetic young woman exclaimed.

"Señora, please understand me. You have families. Go and see to your people, so that they can tend to you. If you don't return home, you risk having your relatives going out to search for you. We don't know what the coming hours will bring. There might be more fighting, maybe they'll cut off the lights and telephones. You yourselves have said that we must *live*, not die for our country. Protect yourselves. Go, please, I beg of you, no matter what you may want."

The unarmed crowd, like a herd in a storm, deserted the field where a shadow descended like a black blanket.

The priest and nuns shuffled down the hallway praying the sorrowful mysteries of the rosary out loud. After the final amen, the night with its frozen stars watched over the large earth, already bereft of expressions and embraces.

Velia Calvimontes was born in Cochabamba, Bolivia, in 1935, in a home where books were prevalent and writing was common. Both her parents were writers; her mother, Flora Salinas, is considered the first woman author of pedagogical materials for elementary schools in Bolivia. Velia Calvimontes followed in her mother's footsteps, graduating with a degree in education and working for a number of years as a professor of languages.

Calvimontes knew from an early age that she wanted to be a writer, but it was not until 1963, when she was twenty-eight and living in Chicago, that she actually began to write. Calvimontes credits an unnerving experience for her initial motivation: "One night my husband and I were returning from the theater, and we were walking through an area where I had never been before. I saw children sleeping on the cold ground in winter, covered with paper and cardboard. I felt a series of emotions: annoyance, rage, impotence, because I didn't know what to do. When we arrived home, my husband went to bed and I wrote a short poem. That was one of my first works; I have now written several similar poems of protest."

Calvimontes continues to write poetic prose, for which she has won several awards, including the Premio Jorge Luís Borges in Buenos Aires, Argentina, in 1986. A great part of Calvimontes's literary production is dedicated to children's literature, for which she has also been awarded numerous literary prizes.

Calvimontes's story "Coati 1950," is written specifically for an adult audience and is considered testimonial in nature. Although it is fiction, it could easily be an accurate account of what an ordinary citizen suffers while imprisoned for a minor infraction, or simply for being under suspicion of having committed a crime. The story unfolds in Bolivia with several references to actual places, but the drama so approximates documented histories, that the events may be viewed as universal throughout many Third World countries.

Calvimontes currently lives in Cochabamba where she is active in literary organizations. She was recently honored by the city of Cochabamba as a Distinguished Citizen for her literary production as well as for her contributions to the field of children's literature.

Coati 1950

by Velia Calvimontes

*A*s a doctor, I am accustomed to seeing all kinds of deformations and mutilated appendages. It would take too long and be very tiring to enumerate them all.

However, that hot afternoon when I examined a group of technicians at base camp, I was amazed to see that the last one I examined didn't possess the anatomical part called the gluteus. The area from the hips up to four centimeters below where the thighs begin was virtually covered with a deep crisscross of scars, the same as on his back.

Strange. But the first thing I associated it with, after the initial impact, was the children's game of "maze" where multiple lines randomly describe a series of routes from which one must choose in order to arrive at the place where a child or an animal is safe in its house.

When the man saw my expression, he smiled sadly.

"You and my wife, besides those who did this to me, are the only ones who have seen this."

"It doesn't appear to be due to an accident. Perhaps you were in a concentration camp?"

"No, I spent a year on the island of Coati. Why I was there had nothing to do with politics."

"But how is it possible that they removed your buttocks? Were you very rebellious?"

"Ah, Doctor. So many things happen in this life! For example, the other day I read in the newspaper that in Arabic countries they cut off a thief's left hand; I was thinking that after all is said and done, those thieves haven't suffered what I have. What do you think I did?"

I looked at him, somewhat electrified, but only succeeded in shaking my head in a gesture of bewilderment.

"Well, I stole three or four pieces of clothing for my brothers and myself, nothing fancy, you understand. I was probably about seventeen years old then."

"The law protecting minors prohibits them from being sent to jail or any kind of prison."

"It was 1950, and that law surely didn't exist at that time. Do you want me to tell you about it?"

"All right, go on while I examine you. Since you're the last one, we have some time."

"On January 23, 1950, I was put behind bars in Cochabamba. As I told you, my crime was having stolen two sweaters and a pair of pants. I had six younger brothers and sisters.

No matter how my parents tried to obtain my freedom by emphasizing my age to the authorities, the lack of connections and money made their attempts useless. To help pay for food and to keep myself occupied, I worked with another convict making carnival masks. I remember looking at the masks, some amusing, others grotesque, and my eyes would fill with tears when I thought about my situation. I was holding in my hands something that would provide joy and pleasure for others. During that whole season I had time to reflect on the actions that caused me to be there, and I firmly promised myself that I would not repeat them. I was profoundly sorry and my shame was sincere.

At the beginning of March, when my hopes of leaving jail were increasing, I was sentenced to the island of Coati along with other inmates. I had no idea what that meant; however, it was not long before I heard reports about that cursed island, surrounded as I was by experienced thieves and delinquents dedicated to the most diverse criminal activities.

The reports made me tremble. Paralyzed with fear, I made a futile attempt to escape. As punishment, the guards took turns kicking and punching me until they left me unconscious.

The thirteenth of March, at dawn, all the condemned prisoners were forced into a line and they had us climb into a truck, all the while insulting us and striking us with the butts of their rifles.

I was not able to say good-bye to my mother, who had risen at dawn to see me leave, or even to hug her. The truck turned the corner and I was able to see her hand waving a silent and desolate farewell.

I cried uncontrollably, feeling no shame, with all the sadness and anguish of my seventeen years. It wasn't simply self pity that I felt, but knowing that at home they would miss my small contributions of money, since before going to jail, I had worked as a carpenter's apprentice. I was sure that with everything that had happened to me in those two months of incarceration, I had more than paid for my sins. How foolish I was to have had such hopes!

During that time I barely had any hair on my face, my beard had not yet begun to grow. Why were they sending me to a place where only the lowest prisoners were sent? I didn't deserve that. Only God and my mother knew the deep remorse I was feeling.

They loaded us onto a boxcar and we left at 9:00 in the morning. Luckily, I had twenty pesos and a blanket. From the looks of it, I was the only one who felt remorseful. The others demonstrated their happiness in various ways; it seemed that once they found themselves outside the four walls of the jail, they imagined themselves free, or was it that the illusion of freedom was enough for them? I never was able to comprehend the reason for their attitude, which I found misplaced.

I watched my money closely, as if that meager amount meant life or death. I remember that I barely spent three pesos to buy food during the day, although I was dying of hunger.

A companion in misfortune who was seated next to me bought a plate heaped with food. It was a meat stew with potatoes and rice. The inviting aroma which rose from the plate made my mouth water. As my mouth filled with saliva, I consoled myself by swallowing it slowly, savoring it, seasoned by what I could discern out of the corner of my eye.

Finally, the afternoon heat and the rocking movement of the train put me to sleep for an hour or two.

When I woke up, the others were sleeping. Hunger was furiously gnawing at me. I looked around; my neighbor was snoring loudly.

Because he had been eating so greedily, he had dropped some food on his clothes and on the floor. Afraid that I would wake him and perhaps arouse his anger—I was the only boy there—with infinite care, I picked the crumbs from his clothes and ate the remaining grains of dry rice. Thus, I completed my meal for that day.

We arrived in Oruro at sunset. The guards led us to some barracks, and kicking us all the way, they locked us in a cell; twenty-four beings crowded together like animals awaiting slaughter. The next day we continued our trip to La Paz. I felt as if I had traveled the entire world.

In that city another dismal jail awaited our arrival.

I felt like an orphan in every sense, especially like an orphan of human justice. I was forced to sell my blanket for forty pesos, money which disappeared in a few days, just like water through open fingers. The wind and the cold were my only nourishment. The cobblestone pavement was my bed.

The March wind and I formed part of the group of forty men destined for the island of Coati.

We traveled by night in a truck. With the first rays of dawn we arrived at the Tiquina Canal. We boarded a ship, and during the journey, rain was the cloak that covered my body. Desperate because of my situation, I felt it would be better to drown. I was getting ready to jump overboard, but a guard guessed my intentions and stopped me. They handcuffed me and brutally beat me. My body and soul were numb; I remember nothing but the words, 'We're here.'

We got off the boat and they made us line up on the shore of the island so they could search us to make sure we weren't carrying any weapons. Then, as a welcome—which it was, an official stressed—they had us dive into the icy water dressed as we were. When we got out, they searched us again to see if we were carrying money or anything of value. Since I had no money, they made me strip and then gave me fifty lashes with a whip. When they confirmed that I also did not have a change of clothing or any blankets, they gave me another fifty. Many who received a similar punishment passed out. To make them recover they were thrown into the water. They had us line up for a third time to take roll call. Perhaps the fear of being thrown into that icy liquid gave me the strength to remain nearly upright. Blood flowed from the hundred wounds like a hundred slender threads and formed a thin, flesh-colored curtain over my back.

We got dressed, and without a bite to eat, we spent the first night on the bare floor of a cell, wrapped in our wet clothing. Some were fortunate enough to cover and warm themselves with their blankets.

The daily routine began. At five in the morning a voice would shout: 'Line up to shower.' We had to swim 50 yards. Those who couldn't do it because of some disability were forced to remain in neck-deep water for two hours. Some could not tolerate the cold: they either cramped up or froze. Several times I saw bubbles and a brief thrashing about which indicated that their punishment had ended.

Our executioners—there is no other word that better describes them, some of them perpetually carried a whip, others had a rifle resting on their shoulders—would say every morning, between laughter and crude expressions, that 'We had to take a morning bath so we could begin the work day clean.'

After the 'bath' there was breakfast—hot sugar water with a piece of cornbread. That meal was somewhat like having to swallow a pill.

Until noon, our work consisted of transporting fifty enormous stones to a spot some two kilometers away. On the first day I was barely able to gather fifteen stones. My punishment was swift: twenty-four lashes, a 'bath,' and the loss of my right to go to the mess hall. With my buttocks bloodied, the water made me feel as if I were being savagely slashed with a knife.

Once, another prisoner noticed that I was unable to gather the required number of stones. He took pity on me and attempted to give me some of his. Unfortunately, the watchful eye of the guard observed the maneuver. He yelled wildly asking for help. The guards made us both stretch out on the ground and the cracks of the whip began their macabre dance. When the guards had finished their work, exhausted and sweating, one of them commented: 'This exercise is good for warming you up in this chilly weather, don't you agree?'

The days passed, then weeks and months. I was never able to fulfill my quota of stones, it was simply beyond my physical capability. With the exertion of hauling stones, my wounds, which were not yet completely healed, opened again.

When the sun reached its zenith, my body would break down trembling. This preceded the panic that would overtake me. I don't know how I kept from going crazy, Doctor.

My companions began to disappear. Weakness wreaked the same

damage as stomach infections and dysentery. When the prisoners became very ill, they would lock them in a special room until their hearts stopped beating. They expired with indescribable suffering, for they were denied even a glass of water to relieve their thirst.

There are no words in the human language that can give meaning to the attitude of those beings who behaved worse than animals in the treatment of their equals. Others, who were healthy and able to tolerate more, but who possibly possessed a more lengthy criminal record, mysteriously disappeared; the guards commented that they had thrown them into the lake.

The casualties, something natural in that sinister place, continued uninterrupted, one or two a week.

The pain penetrates deep into my mind and flesh like a piercing drill when I remember one particular occasion. It was lunch time, and as usual, I was starving. The daily meal consisted of flour soup—the meat shone in its absence—with dirty unpeeled potatoes, sometimes worm-infested. I stuck my finger in my mouth to remove a piece of dirt that had become lodged between my teeth, and I naturally spat a little. The guard who was constantly watching us, thought I was refusing the food and, assisted by another guard, let loose with an inhumane beating. The whip rose and fell, biting into my flesh. When sweat and exhausted muscles prevented one of them from continuing, the other jailer would relieve him. My bloodied buttocks exploded like cactus flowers. All around me, splattered blood and pieces of flesh were mute testimony to my torture. They left my body there, like a bloodless rag.

I wanted only to die. Because of my condition, they excused me from hauling rocks. One day they put me in charge of collecting firewood. I didn't return to the barracks, I attempted to escape by fleeing in the opposite direction. I was spurred on by the idea that when my captors saw me, they would carry out the rule of flight and shoot. But no, instead they dragged me away with them.

My desperation had no limits. What further torture awaited me if they would punish us so mercilessly for the slightest infraction?

This time it was not the whip that unleashed its fury on me; instead, blows from clubs rained down on me, causing me to lose consciousness.

When I recovered my senses—I don't know how long I was

unconscious—I told myself that my days were numbered. I could not move; my efforts to sit up were in vain; my demise was imminent, I reasoned. Others who had found themselves in this condition had been left to their own devices in a room where only dead men exited.

I envisioned my grave, the tossing of my body into a hole and being covered with earth and straw as I had witnessed so many times before. Believing that my time had come, I offered up a prayer, more from gratitude than to beg for clemency, I believe.

Unexpectedly, my luck changed. They began to take care of me, bringing me water and food. They removed me from that fateful cell, and within a few days, they announced that I was free, that I could return to my family as soon as I was strong enough.

I couldn't believe it. Was I dreaming or was I delirious? The food improved daily and I tasted meat for the first time in many months. There was no explanation for this sudden change.

About a week or so after the miraculous change, they gave me some money so I could travel to Cochabamba; that is how a few of us fortunate ones left that ill-fated island.

Later, I put two and two together. The words 'they say there are accusations' and 'there's going to be an inspection,' gave me a clue as to what was going on. Most likely, reports had somehow leaked concerning the manner in which we were treated. At the root of it was a change in the rules concerning the treatment of the prisoners. It's possible that while reviewing the list they discovered that I was the only minor, and in order to not be held responsible, they set me free along with the others who had not committed any serious offenses.

Twenty-three years have passed, Doctor. I don't know if I would have preferred for them to cut off one of my hands like they do in Arabic countries, or to have spent that time in captivity.

Tell me, Doctor, why, when a poor person commits a relatively minor crime, such as I did, is he so severely punished? And when a rich man steals, no matter how many millions, the law looks the other way and allows him to go free with impunity? Another question, Doctor. What good is that piece of parchment called the Declaration of Human Rights? It doesn't exist for the poor and unfortunate, does it? Those famous 'Rights' which are so carefully framed and hanging in offices and appear in large letters in newspaper headlines are only for show.

What do you think, Doctor?"

At that moment, I couldn't find an appropriate response. I was barely able to say this:

"You should be satisfied, friend. You passed the physical exam with no problems," and I patted him affectionately on the shoulder and added, "life has some unfathomable facets for which there sometimes are no answers."

That night I was unable to sleep because I found the answers to his questions, and they were absolutely unacceptable.

A testimonial.

Nayla Chehade Durán, the daughter of Lebanese immigrants to Colombia, was born in Cali in 1953. In 1962 her family moved to the Dominican Republic, where the country's dictator, Rafael L Trujillo, had been assassinated the year before. It was there that Chehade Durán received her elementary and secondary education in Catholic schools run by Franciscan nuns. Chehade Durán feels that the ten years she spent in the Dominican Republic, precisely because it was during a post-dictator era, were decisive in the awakening of her literary ambitions. She recalls writing what she calls "little novels" with her best friend and clandestinely reading books that the nuns would never have assigned.

Everything that Chehade Durán writes is infused with a Caribbean flavor, physical as well as emotional. A number of her stories deal specifically with the aftermath of Trujillo's dictatorship. She describes the thirty years when Trujillo was in office as a reign of terror, a time when he maintained absolute control over the country. He was considered the "Supreme General," the "Father of the New Country," and "the Benefactor," in charge of watching over the well-being of his children. He was an omnipresent patriarch who rewarded those loyal to him, but who mercilessly punished those who dared to disobey.

Through her stories "The Vigil" and "The Visit," Chehade Durán literarily explores the populist support that Trujillo enjoyed in the Dominican Republic, viewed through the eyes of her feminine protagonists. All of Chehade Durán's protagonists are women, their voices anonymous and marginal, each relating her own personal drama hidden from the public eye. These women are marred beings, scarred by the tragedy that gripped their country, a tragedy equal to those experienced by many others in Latin America.

In the story "The Vigil," we are allowed to view the lives of young girls, victims of ideological manipulation, where the patriarchal paradigm responds to the image and the expectations created by the regime and its tyranny. The young student who dares to ignore the advice and warnings of her religious keepers suffers her due fate when she dies from a botched abortion.

In "The Visit," Chehade Durán highlights the ambiguity of the relationship between the dictator and a large sector of his subjects who possess few tools for critical articulation, but who nonetheless possess the necessary lucidity to detect this ambivalence. A fortune teller who has been chosen by the dictator to read his future in the cards alternately praises and condemns him, as she struggles to overcome the awe his physical presence creates.

In 1993 Chehade Durán was awarded the Francisco de Paula Santander Grant by the Colombian Institute of Culture in the category of short story to finish work on a collection that will include "The Visit" and "The Vigil." She is currently working on a trilogy that includes tales told by her grandmothers.

The Vigil

by Nayla Chehade Durán

For Diógenes Noboa Guerrero

*P*erhaps if she had been more obedient and appreciative, the nuns were heard to say, she would have avoided much of the punishment she had to tolerate, and surely she would have avoided the misfortune of such a premature death. Long Sunday afternoons were spent biting our nails, listening to the darkened voices that spilled out of the little box radio, and anxiously awaiting Olga's swaying entrance as she carried her tray filled with red drinks and humble pastries. And we waited for Serena's hands, which knew how to skillfully arrange the black waves of her hair, how to uncover new brilliance in the oily green paint on the walls, those hands that replaced the wilted flowers in the chapel with fresh ones, or were pricked by the needle in its forced journey of mending and hemming. I think now that she wasn't beautiful, at least not as beautiful as we believed her to be then, when each one of her gestures represented for us a powerful longing for the unattainable. I dare to assert, however, if her road to misfortune began with those nocturnal visits, with those hurried hours of clandestine encounters, she managed to live more in that brief lapse of time than we will probably live in a span of many years.

It's true that she never wanted us to be like her, nor did she expect us to imitate her. She simply told us her secrets when she felt like it, for the pleasure and necessity of being heard. She liked to talk, to gratify herself with the inflections of her own voice, and to allow herself to be carried along by her predisposition for intimacy. It stemmed from sharing a room, a large room, with four windows made of wood and glass which looked out onto the color of the tamarinds and mango trees in the back patio. We five boarders slept together in a room; two fell asleep easily and slept soundly. They were younger than we were and never showed any interest in Serena's stories, or perhaps they were never awake when the night seemed to stand still and she answered Delfín's call, radiant, fearless, with no uneasiness to interfere with her emotions, with no inkling of doubt to undermine her impetuosity. Even during those numerous days of confession, when Isaura and I burned without clemency in the fires of guilt as we approached Father Efraín's voracious ear trembling, Serena ignored the inquisitional stares of Sister Eufrasia and remained seated on the edge of the bench, her hands quiet in her lap and her gaze transparent.

Every afternoon after six o'clock prayers, it was Serena's duty to turn out the chapel lights and lock the front door. The back door and the door to the sacristy, which opened to the street through a passageway overwhelmed by lemon trees and white rosebushes, were closed by Father Efraín in the afternoons when he left. It was very easy for Serena to take the key that Sister Asunción kept hanging next to the image of San Francisco shepherding the sheep, and leave the way clear for Delfín, with no more complicity than the vehemence of her desire and the smiles we wore while waiting for her in the dining room. She descended the stairs calmly, and she spoke with the same naturalness as always about her history exam or that long ago weekend when her grandmother had taken her to see her father. We never saw any signs of absence or remoteness in her expression, nor did we observe any trembling in her hands which might announce the proximity of her vigil.

We were not allowed to go to bed until nine o'clock, the preestablished time. After finishing dinner, many times our lives seemed to stagnate between leftovers and burned grease, while we helped Olga and Sister Baudelina put the kitchen in order. Later we had to arrange our blue and white uniforms for the next morning and give the plants some water to help ward off the sun's glare. Large and green, the potted jasmines and creepers in the interior patio grew insolently toward the light, and the earthy humidity they emitted slapped us in the face when water fell on them. Serena seemed to enjoy this chore the rest of us detested. We were intimidated by the absence of voices, the pounding of crickets, the faint light, the stone arms of the Redeemer Savior, and the empty rooms and infinite hallways, all so remote and distant from everything that they caused us to fear our very existence.

She never asked us to wait for her, and as soon as we finished, we would climb up to the second floor to rest, utterly terrified. From there we could see how she turned out the few remaining lights and lighted the small lamp near the main entrance, next to the portrait of the *Generalísimo*. Then she would climb the stairs two by two, almost always humming one of the latest songs, oblivious to the power of those eyes watching her move up the stairs, untouched by the arrogance of his two-cornered hat and the thickness of his eyebrows, completely safe from his help and from his kindness.

Mulatto, mulatto, nearly black, Delfín Flores, mulatto from the capital, back patio and coal-burning stove, shared latrine and curtains instead of doors, branch from a guava tree used for a bat, wad of string that becomes a ball, amazement in his eyes as they watch the caravan, the shine off the cars that pull greetings from those watching, blessings from all who sway under the sun. Mulatto, mulatto, almost black, buttocks round and firm, close-shaved hair cut two centimeters above the ear, and a khaki uniform. Mulatto, mulatto, almost black, Delfín Flores to serve the Jefe and God in any corner of the country, escorter of processions and tracker of subversives, there is nothing greater than the Benefactor and no other love but Serena. Army private, Delfín Flores, perpetual agony of nights on guard, statue of San Francisco that watches him enter, ocean's dampness that is always with him, hands of Serena that feel his body, Serena's breathing which fills him with life, Serena's nipples that blossom in his mouth, Serena's bouquet which comes untied in his lips.

The nights when Delfín came were endless for Isaura and me. Beneath the mosquito net, outlined in the semidarkness, we could imagine Serena's arms extended over her pillow and the profile of her body wrapped in a white cotton bathrobe. When the wooden blades of the fan pushed her words toward us, what we so dreaded invariably happened, and slowly we succumbed to the fear of imagining the unimaginable, of sensing the impossible. Sister Eufrasia's shouts of warning in religion class remained crushed at the base of a precipice for several minutes, and the ferocious ragings of desire that Father Efraín had so often warned us about, finally completely devoured us. At the arranged time, Serena would lift the mosquito net, take the sheet she kept folded at her side and say good-bye to us, giving a festive gesture of farewell with her hand. Isaura and I remained motionless, desolate, watching how she disappeared, seeming to float. We were incapable of breathing or of saying anything, suddenly at the mercy of ourselves and the heat, of the stale air from the fan, and of the tranquil sleep of our roommates.

We never knew what time Serena returned to bed, because sleep would finally overcome us. When the bell woke us, light was already flooding the room, and the mirror on the dresser and the bronze crucifix shone like always as Serena stretched unhurriedly. At that hour, everything seemed so simple and mundane, like what had happened the night before might have been a dream. There was no other certainty besides the heat and the pressure of a day like any other at boarding school, complete with prayers for the health of the Benefactor and afflicted by acts of faith and contrition in the gloomy confines of our classroom. We never dared to insinuate anything. Nor did Serena seem interested in alluding to her secret encounters during that time. On those mornings, Isaura and I spied on her every movement. We watched, engrossed, as she smoothed down with the palms of her hands the pleats of her blue uniform, which she already had on. As she gave the last touches to her bed, we searched in her mulatta smile, on her meaty lips, for traces of her late night lovemaking or hidden signs of her passion. But all we saw appear were large, white teeth, which she constantly exhibited without inhibition.

Light-skinned mulatta, nearly white, Serena Aguiar, tinkling laughter and just-turned sixteen. Light-skinned mulatta, nearly white, hair like a blackened sponge, breasts like green limes. Mulatta washed nearly white, house of blue and red wood, floor of cement and dust, prayers from her grandmother in the other bed. Serena del Carmen, pretty little girl, ten cents worth of tomato sauce to prepare lunch, the

Three Wise Men who lose their way and river sadness that carries the ships away. Mulatta, light, light, Serena Aguiar, innocence conceived in El Inocente, recognized by force, recognition by the colonel, the colonel's concession, thirteen broken years, and a Catholic school paid for on the other coast, Serena, nothing more important than escaping from boarding school, and the love of Delfín. Serena del Carmen Aguiar, light-skinned mulatta, nearly white, semidarkness of the hallways that obscures her face, warmth of the night that deepens her breathing, genuflection on the run and an altar lamp to light the way. Serena, so serene, glass door that opens without a key and a gray terrace with a warm floor. Serena del Carmen Aguiar, Delfín's embrace which completely dissolves her, Delfín's breathing which entirely dampens her, Delfín's tongue which completely soaks her. Serena del Carmen, light-skinned mulatta, earth-shaking tremor which quickly revives her, Delfín's heart which swims between her breasts, ocean and sky that become one.

The nuns had been anxious that Sunday afternoon when we pushed open the bathroom door and saw Serena lying on the floor, drowned in her own blood. Sister Concepción had to twice write the words MOTHER and MODEL in glitter on the sign she planned to place at the entrance to the theater, and Sister Eufrasia didn't seem satisfied with any of the satin tunics she planned to use in the celebrations that were approaching in honor of the Virgen. But it wasn't Serena's death which prevented those celebrations. The same Monday as her burial, the capital was a beehive of activity due to the news of an air strike intended to overthrow the government, and classes were cancelled. None of us was able to understand then how it was possible to hate the man who had given us everything. Much later, when the story of the insurgents began to be clandestinely told amid the enthusiasm of *rumbas* and *merengues*, when I learned to ask questions, the memory of Serena continued to be patched together. And many times I wondered if she continued to be for Isaura that same warm shadow that I had tried so many times in vain to frighten off during those years, and if Delfín, whom we only saw smiling sadly, rifle in hand, in front of the curtain of palm trees in a photograph, might have survived the terror of that era and had enough strength to call forth any memories of it.

When Serena returned the May afternoon that we found her dead, no one could have foreseen the misfortune in the emptiness of her eyes. No one could have foretold her shouts for help or the pressure of the paper bag containing her clothing held against her belly, nor were we capable of noticing the hot, acrid smell of blood in the shine of perspiration that bathed her face. We didn't see her grandmother in the receiving room like other times, and Serena barely greeted us when we approached to receive her. She claimed to have the symptoms of a cold and requested permission not to come down to the dining room. Later, she went up to our room, stair by stair, her steps short and her right hand grasping the railing. Several hours after that moment, when our eyes were seared with the image of her, immobile, kissing the bathroom floor and warming the cold of the tiles with her hair, Serena headed to the street in a military hospital gurney, completely covered from the sight of the living, en route to the capital.

The following day, the heat woke us and the entire room smelled of disinfectant. The unreal clarity of the morning undid the torpor of sleeping pills, and with horror, Isaura and I looked at one another in the mirror of truth. When Sister Eufrasia entered, wearing the same dark dignity she used to address us with in religion classes, she sat down on the same bed that we had anxiously watched on so many nights and she explained Serena's death to us as the result of a poorly-attended hemorrhage, aggravated by a history of deficient coagulation and circulatory problems. She told us that our families had requested that we not be allowed to go out, and that Sister Concepción and Sister Caridad were accompanying Serena's grandmother to the wake. There were no deep interrogations or exhaustive inquiries, only if lately we had heard Serena mention the name of some Delfín, or if we had noticed anything strange in her behavior. The sister's eyes were wandering and her gestures erratic, and perhaps only Isaura and I could perceive the veiled recrimination that rested in each of her words of sympathy. And surely Isaura also detached herself effortlessly from the sticky pronunciation of *z*s and from the wet whistle of the *c*s of that absent Franciscan, to continue thinking, as I was, where Serena was at that moment when her grandmother should be embracing her lifeless body, where she had been the night before, while she travelled for two salted hours, her face shrouded against the ocean breeze, eyes closed to the silvery trembling of the coconut and sea grape groves, where her soul and her love for Delfín were. But we allowed nothing to show besides a few hot tears of pain and fear. Nor did we answer when the sister caressed the knots on the belt of her habit and with a sigh told us that it had not been possible to locate Serena's mother in New York; I continued thinking, and perhaps Isaura did too, about what was going to happen to Delfín's promises of marriage, to the house that they were going to buy in the capital when he became a captain, and to the children they were going to have. And we didn't even want to tell her how much Serena had dreamed about seeing her father when Sister Eufrasia told us that he would pay for the funeral expenses and the flowers, but that he would not be present either, because he was heading the mission in charge of capturing the rebels. She asked nothing else, not even what we were going to do from then on with our inner trembling that paralyzed our voices, or how we were going to be able to tolerate the blaze emanating from the chapel's stained glass windows as it shone into our eyes at high noon while Father Efraín presided over Serena's memorial mass. Then, she talked to us about the power of prayer while she burned our faces with the heat of her embrace. She asked us to pray continually for Serena's soul and pleaded for our discretion, to avoid harmful comments. Before leaving the room, she announced that the school would no longer offer boarding the following year. When she said this, Isaura and I renewed with a look our secret vow of eternal friendship without suspecting that although we might be burdened by the same effects of that time in a number of ways, life had already traced very different paths for us, and we would never see one another again.

Light-skinned mulatta, almost white, Serena del Carmen Aguiar, terror that darkens her expression, needle that pierces her heart, moistness of the day that soaks her thighs, nightly lethargy that clouds her soul, thirty days of waiting and no sign of blood. Serena, light-skinned mulatta, almost white, burning within, scaldings in her breasts, Sunday noon completely wilts her, inner trembling that withers her all, Serena del Carmen Aguiar, rag doll walking with a broken belly. Mulatta, light, light, almost white, paleness of death, cardboard suitcase, three romance novels and a little plastic mirror, pink lipstick and a Sunday dress, blue and white uniform and a pair of patent-leather shoes, Serena, final inventory, six letters from Delfín and a dedicated photograph. Serena, so serene, pale mulatta, almost white, whiteness of death, transparency of death, living room wake and grandmother's tears, coffee and cookies with guava jelly, sadness on the river that carries the ships away.

The Visit

by Nayla Chehade Durán

So he could open up the route to Santa Clara and to San Miguel Arcángel and to help him overcome his enemies with the power of his sword, he had asked me to commend him, yes sir, and right there, next to Saint Marta la Dominadora, he sat down so I could read him the cards. Even though the eleven o' clock heat seared the zinc tiles on the roof, I shivered all inside to see him there at my side, breathing deeply, full of brilliance and medals, bathed in essences, with sweat slowly sliding down and breaking trails on his dusty face. Even though many years were yet to pass before the bullets would pierce his chest, from that moment on, I could see the sign of betrayal on the dagger that stubbornly intermingled in the abundance of gold, and this is what I told him, swallowing hard, entrusting myself to the spirits, seeing out of the corner of my eye the thick veil of his eyelashes, the gentle look in his eyes. But he barely smiled, and he began to mop his neck and forehead with his linen handkerchief, embroidered and perfumed, and then he looked at the ceiling and told me my roof was caving in on me. I didn't know how to answer, because the little I had was given to me by the saints, what I had was acquired for me by the dead, and I had no idea how I was going to get through the following week while I was out gathering coal to use for cooking.

I was thinking how the heat had gotten worse and Chana hadn't appeared for her herbal bath, when I went running for the door, frightened by the noise. I saw an army truck full of soldiers throwing out red and green signs, piling up sacks of cement, and stirring up chickens in the middle of clouds of dust. A crowd of boisterous people had come out onto their patios to see what was happening. It's true that after a few days my house seemed completely different, and that it was the only one among all of them with a new roof and a decent floor. Even though the only thing we breathed was dust every waking moment, at least I began to hope I would have a pair of winged windows where I could stop once in a while to wait for the illusion of an afternoon breeze. And it's also true that if it hadn't been for him, the altar to my saints would have been eaten by moths. I never would have been able to fix it or to dress the saints in so much satin and lace like what he sent me, all without asking him to, just like the six boxes of dried fish he sent for the offerings to the dead. The last thing I thought about when I found myself at his side was to ask him for anything, and even less to tell him that since the dawn of time the earth's fire had tormented us while we slept and that our insides churned from eating so much plantain at every meal. How was I going to talk to him about those things or tell him that when the latrines backed up we felt as if we were being eaten alive by so many flies and the unbearable stench. I was terrified of contaminating him with my words, of spoiling his perfume by talking to him about such filth. How was I going to tell him that we lived with wrinkled hearts and sad eyes from seeing nothing but scorched scrub brush, from sighing among clouds of dust, if out there in the capital he had all the light of the ocean in front of him, all the clear air to drink in. No, I couldn't tell him anything that day. He had come to the border to take care of the Haitian problem, but he had to see how much oblivion had disheartened us, how much it had dried out the dead earth, because he was capable of at least that and so much more.

Nobody had told me about San Zenón, and nobody had told me about the heads sent trembling through the air, nor about the houses dancing in the sky. Although it happened a long time ago, I saw that with my own eyes, because out there, the rage of the cyclone and the fury of winds seized us. Although it seemed like the city would never be able to live again, he revived it, he didn't allow the ocean to swallow it up, and he knew what he had to do. So that's why I didn't say anything that day when I had him in front of me, that time when

I could have touched him if I had stretched out my arm, while he cut the cards so I could continue my job. My eyes surprised me in the mirrors of his fingernails, all even, all the same, with tender half-moons, without thinking that we were going to spend so many years entertaining sadness with the illusion of his distant accomplishments, fingering his portrait before going to bed, bringing new life to it with little jars of clear water underneath, until finally one day, the first road crossed through our town and electric bulbs illuminated our faces with the joy of their light. We all went out with little flags in our hands to seek blessings for him while we received sacks of flour and butter and the miracle of powdered milk. When we pressed up against one another to see how the school had turned out, the one o'clock sun cracked our skin and clouded our vision, but we managed to make out his wide forehead, his clean and calm face in the whiteness of the statue which we tried to touch without being able to because the soldiers filled our hands with new photographs. After they ordered us to leave the street, a fervor grew in many of us because we suddenly didn't know what to do with so much fabricated happiness, with so many adorned images, and our happiness disappeared when we thought about what was going to happen when they left and we were alone again, extinguished by the heat, sucked dry by the mosquitoes, grasping at hope, wasting away with every candle we lit for the saints, turning into smoke with each stick of incense that we burned to frighten off the bad luck. It wasn't like that day so many years ago when I could have touched him if I had raised my arm, that time when my voice broke while reading his destiny to him in the cards. I couldn't help but wonder why he was in my house, how it was that he had asked my permission to use my rocking chair. He had asked me with such respect, when I was nobody, and every time he felt like it he brought witches from Guayama and priestesses from Haiti so they could work their powers on him. On that day, many of my *comadres* suffered fainting spells in the doorway, and they had to move the men with rifle butts because nobody wanted to be kept from seeing him up close. Nobody wanted to miss touching him and asking him for his blessing. Back then, very few believed what they were beginning to say about him, and almost no one paid attention to the voices that scratched the walls with their stories of death. Since I had never had anyone of my own blood to watch over, and since I've lived devoted to fulfilling my destiny, I had never found myself with my soul so distressed as those who came to tell me their stories, because I've never even had a man to suffer for. We wallowed in our pain together. This was when Anaísa was nervous and angry all the time and I had to humor her; when I was fed-up and haggard and she wouldn't get down off her saddle until she tired of the men and got sick of rum and perfume. They knew they were with me not because she wanted it, because she was the only bandit whore amongst the legion of saints, and I had to follow her orders, so that my blood wouldn't boil in anger and I wouldn't have to live through the fits of hysteria that caused the women who came to me for a cure for their love problems to explode. No sir, I owe everything to my saints and that is my pride. That's why when the day they killed Chana's husband, I again gave thanks for my solitude of so many years. That same night the howls from that woman sounded like a dog giving birth; they woke us all. Those who knew the truth said that they broke him of being brave, for saying that the government was stealing everything, and that with sixty cents a day you couldn't support a family of five. That's how they say it was, and they brought him from far away, from the plantation, stuffed in a sack, and they unloaded him in the doorway with the consolation that the Boss wasn't going to abandon the widow of a treacherous drunk, nor her children, either.

The truth is that it was hard for me to accept those things, to think that what they were saying out there—those who dared, shaking with fear—could be true, and that he was guilty of so much killing and so much abuse like we heard about. And me, who saw him up close that day, so close that I could have touched him if I had lifted my arm, that time when my words escaped me, when I heard the sweetness of his voice, when my senses became confused by the gentleness of his expression. I wouldn't have been capable of accusing him of any-thing, not even of being perverted with women like they claim he was. They say that sometimes he chose them before they began to menstru-ate, and they had to be saved for him until their breasts appeared. And they say that he would mount them many times in one night, and it wasn't only because of fear that they submitted to him, but because they went crazy for him. Me, who saw him up so close that I could have caressed him if I had extended my arm; my saints didn't even matter to me anymore. I can't deny that I was disturbed by the curve of his mouth, and my hair stood on end looking at the dark mound of his mustache. And every time he touched the cards with his fingers, without wanting it to, my mind became fanned like a new flame thinking what it would be like to receive the juices of his body and taste his sweat. That's why I can't say anything, but those who know say that before the bullet pierced his chest, he had already begun to pay for his evilness because he had begun to rot from within, and there were no prayers or medicines that could fix his masculinity. They say he couldn't even use it for urinating anymore, and he wet his pants in front of people. But even so, many believed that it was little suffering for the damage that he had caused, and they said that he deserved to be skinned alive like he had ordered for so many who were put in cages in La Cuarenta. That's where they took María Ramona's son, and she never saw him again because they say he was thrown to the sharks. That's right, that when the moment arrived for burning photographs, when we were smashing statues, she released the rage she had held in for so many years, all the silenced screams for her only son, and she was the one who threw the most stones, and she was the one who more mothers mentioned. Yes sir, I saw it all from my window, because when I heard the shouting and a noise that sounded like the earth opening up, I dragged myself with my stiff leg, and as best as I could, I stood up so I wouldn't miss a thing. There were also many who had twisted up their mouths with incredulity when I told them what I had seen in the cards, screaming, and while they were being overcome by the heat and while they were trying to erase everything that remained in their memories, I could see him, even more alive above the clouds of dust, clean and powerful, with his chest glowing with the brilliance of his honors. And I heard him speaking to me slowly and softly, like that day when I had him so close that I could have fondled him if I had lifted my arm. But I wasn't going to tell anybody that, and even less was I going to tell them that since that moment when the bullets opened his chest and passed through his face, since then, every afternoon he pats my shoulder and asks to borrow my rocking chair. I don't want them saying that I've been helping him with my prayers, or that I want to help him with my pleas and my candles. If everything they say about him isn't a lie, there's nothing I can do, and the truth is that the sadness in his bottomless eyes tells me that there is no hope for his spirit, no sir. But I'm not like others who now curse his name, the same ones who not long ago fell to the ground, possessed by tremors and confused by fear when they learned the news of his death. The truth is that my judgment has not been obscured to the point where I feel that without him we are less than what we were, because we have no hope that someone might remember us, when the scrub brush is stunted by the sun and the breeze dies before it's born. Meanwhile, no one sweeps the dust that saddens the street, and the flies eat the dead strings hanging from the electric lights, while I allow him to use my rocking chair. I let him rock softly so the pain of his condemned soul dissipates, while I break cinnamon sticks for my potions. I then compose, as best I can, what remains of my altar, while I wait for my day to arrive.

Sylvia Diez Fierro was born in Peñablanca, a small town near Valparaíso, Chile. As the daughter of a naval officer, fifteen days after her birth, she began what she calls a nomadic life in which she felt "like a snail with its house on its back and the ocean constantly appearing in its windows." Once Diez Fierro married, she hoped her life would take on some stability. However, her husband was the consulting physician with the Panamerican Organization of Health, and the next eighteen years were filled with frequent moves, with one of the last landing Diez Fierro and her family in Maryland for several years.

In 1988, Diez Fierro returned to Chile where she began to write. "I had always had a secret desire to narrate stories, but my family obligations had made this difficult. Despite my itinerant life, with so much realistic material to draw from, nothing I write is real. I have no explanation as to where my characters come from; they take on life in the corners of my imagination, and I simply direct them as I would a puppet, at times being surprised by their undirected actions."

Diez Fierro's story, "The Sailor's Wife," combines fantastic elements in a tale, that until the very end, seems completely based in reality, detailing a family's cruelty and intolerance toward their son's new bride. The twist at the end is unexpected yet delightful, surprising readers with the magic realism that seems to exist so comfortably in Latin America. In 1993 "The Sailor's Wife" won an honorable mention in the Second Latin American Competition of the Short Story Written by Women.

Diez Fierro's second story anthologized here, "We Must Keep Fanning the Master," utilizes black humor to underscore the precarious existence of peasant workers on a large hacienda. Utilizing their wits and special cunning, which years of subjugation have sharpened, the workers are able to "perpetuate" the life of their master, which ultimately will allow them to remain in their comfortable surroundings.

Diez Fierro has written some twenty unpublished stories, an unpublished novel titled *Puede Ud. llamarme O'Malley*, and has recently published a collection of short stories with three other authors titled *Pulsos Cardinales*.

The Sailor's Wife

by Silvia Diez Fierro

*T*he beach was deserted, as usual. Mooring the sailboat in the dark was no problem for me. I knew the dock, the beach, and the house surrounded by shadows like the back of my hand.

My steps were slow as I approached the house. I knew no one was there because I had seen Dionisia, the Jamaican woman, when she entered the ocean, following the sailboat that carried my grandmother and me.

I saw her disappear when the water engulfed her. I didn't care. She had always been a thorn in my side.

She was a stocky black woman, quiet and ugly. She adored my grandmother and never left her side.

When I was small, I surprised Dionisia in her room on her knees, surrounded by burning candles. She was chanting strange words in a guttural voice that didn't seem to be her own. Since then, the distance between us increased and I grew up believing she was a witch.

The death of the captain—my grandfather—was very recent, and that's why I had remained in the house. Sitting in front of the window, I contemplated the ocean during the daytime, and at night, I felt it pulling at the sand, shaking the sailboat tied to the dock, or silently rocking those who slept in its depths.

How many days? I don't know. One morning I heard my grandfather's lawyers knocking at the door; they asked to see his widow. They needed to read the will to her and to get her orders for the legal proceedings.

When I informed them that she had died and that at her request she had been buried at sea, they demanded to see the death certificate and the name of the doctor who had attended to her.

I had nothing, nothing except my pain and this vacuum of time of days and hours.

They arrested me. But only for twenty-four hours because my family took charge of presenting the medical certificates and of giving the necessary explanations, including a document in which my grandmother expressed her wish to be buried at sea.

"You understand," they said. "She was a sailor's wife and she wanted to be buried in the ocean, like him."

My family then decided that I should travel for awhile.

They thought I was leaving, but I went to the big house on the beach.

Now I am here, surrounded by silence, the whisper of the waves, and loneliness.

I am accompanied only by my memories and the need to write this story, which is also a part of my life.

My grandfather was a sailor. The keel of his sailboat left scars on every ocean in an era when the wind was still a blessing for the men of the sea.

My family had always lived on a hill facing the bay. From the house surrounded by windows, you could see his ship entering the port with its sails full of wind.

Great-grandmother Rosa, his mother, told me that he returned from one of his trips with a wife, but she gave me few details.

Everyone went down to the boat to meet her. She was not to anyone's liking, and they advised my grandfather to take her elsewhere to live, to a faraway seashore. It would be healthier for her, they felt.

My grandfather bought a solitary beach. He fenced it and built a house filled with windows that faced the ocean. He surrounded it with gardens and a dock.

He also bought a small sailboat.

During his long absences, Dionisia, a black Jamaican woman, took care of Sarah, that was my grandmother's name, and when my mother was born, Rosa said that she would raise her.

My grandfather took my mother to her, because neither Rosa nor anyone else in the family ever visited the big house on the beach.

My parents died in an accident when I was a baby and Rosa and the family took charge of me. But each time my grandfather returned from a trip, he took me with him to the house on the beach, where pelicans, sea lions, and elephant seals lived and frolicked in their rookeries.

And that's how my childhood progressed; as a vigil from the house near the port, watching for my grandfather's boat to appear and spending marvelous seasons on the beach.

I loved my grandmother Sarah. She was beautiful, not very tall; her hair held reflections of the moon, and her green eyes disappeared into the shadows of her eyelashes. She was sweet and happy. The time I spent with her was the most precious thing that I possessed.

The Jamaican woman bathed my grandmother, combed her hair, and dressed her in long tunics. Sometimes she would take her out for a stroll in her wheelchair, and sometimes, but not very often, my grandmother would move about slowly, with the help of two crutches.

At night, when they thought I was asleep, my grandfather would carry her in his arms and they would go down to the beach.

Once I followed them. I hid in the rocks and I watched as he combed her hair with a gold comb that he had bought for her in India, with rubies encrusted in the handle. He then placed barrettes made of shells in her hair. She was singing softly. A few watchful sea gulls approached, and several sea lions perched on the rocks and remained very still.

Then my grandfather took off his clothes and removed my grandmother's tunic. Carrying her in his arms, they entered the sea. They swam for a long time while I listened to their laughter, unable to move, feeling that I was part of a secret that no one had ever told me.

Since that night on the beach, I loved my grandparents even more, but I never said anything about it. The next day, I remember that Sarah, sitting in her chair, hugged me very tightly. Ignoring Dionisia's ugly face, I buried mine in my grandmother's hair, perfumed with the scent of seaweed.

During that time, my grandfather stopped sailing and dedicated himself entirely to his wife. On rare occasions he would leave, but only to see me during my vacations or when a family matter required his presence.

And so I grew and became a woman among stories of the sea, my grandfather's journeys, and tales of dolphins and tritons.

I was twenty years old when, during one of his trips to the port, my grandfather had a heart attack and died. The entire family sailed through the port on a single ship, and we buried my grandfather at sea, like we believed we should do with a sailor.

His mother Rosa, who was then very old, put me in charge of relaying the news to Sarah.

It wasn't necessary. When I arrived at the big house on the beach, Dionisia's nose was red and her eyes were swollen. Sarah, seated in her chair facing the ocean, more serene and beautiful than ever, allowed her gaze to wander over the waves.

We remained in silence, holding hands. At nightfall, between tears and whispers, Dionisia bathed my grandmother and dressed her in a beautiful tunic. She asked me to comb her hair with the gold comb. The black woman lifted my grandmother in her arms and we went down to the beach. Only my steps echoed on the dock. She placed my grandmother in the sailboat. I unfurled the sails, and helped by the oars, I put out to sea. I could clearly see the Jamaican woman entering the ocean; the last thing to disappear were her eyes, riveted on the sailboat.

I went very far out. The moon and the stars shone above our heads. When I brought in the sails, the small boat stopped. I helped Sarah remove her tunic, and without embracing me, only smiling sweetly, she slipped from the side of the boat and swam away, without hurrying. I allowed the tide to take me back to the beach.

At this part of the story, I prefer to destroy what I have written and save for myself alone the memories and the last image I have of my grandmother. As she swam away, the moon reflected off the scales of her beautiful fishtail.

We Must Keep Fanning
the Master

by Silvia Diez Fierro

*T*he fan made of palm leaves rises and falls, slicing the air which gathers itself again, leaving no trace of scars.

Zacarías knows how to do it, because as soon as his arms were strong enough, they gave him the job of fanning Master Rubén. A fly lands on the Master's belly. He watches it walk over the wrinkle of his belly button. It climbs and descends on the shiny skin, and in front of a drop of sweat, it stops. It then moves its legs, cleaning its wings and then passing them over its head.

If it bothers the Master, Zacarías has no way of knowing it, because he doesn't speak. For as long as he can remember, the Master has never moved.

They say he had a difficult birth, leaving his mother filled with pain, and there was no one who was able to stop the tepid flow of a stream that lasted two days, until it left her face without color and her body without life.

The son grew a little every year, and each month, became a little fatter. Zacarías thinks that he was around ten years old when he grabbed the fan for the first time and saw Rubén up close. Everyone in the house is attentive to him because they say that the old Master has warned them of the punishment that will befall those responsible if his son is not kept clean or if he finds a mark on his body.

Aunt Tomasa, who was his nanny, decided to feed him through a cane of bamboo after he lost the strength to suck on the bottle and little by little began to lose the ability to move.

Not even his eyes move, thinks the boy, who allows the fly to wander lightly over the Master's arms and legs, and then on his face. It enters his nose and outlines his eyes, over and over again.

The noise from the old Master's boots on the white tile floor causes the boy to shoo the fly away and reinitiate the fan's rhythm. He hears the Master stop, like he does every time he passes through the hallway where his hunting trophies hang. Every year he adds a new one, and he puts Uncle Jaco, who is famous throughout the region, in charge of it. His steps pound the floor again and he enters the room. As large as the Master is, his size still does not compare with Rubén's. In one hand he carries a riding whip, and with his other he tousles his son's hair. He looks at him without saying anything, then he leaves. And so it goes, day after day, whether the air is light or a storm is approaching. Until one day, no one knows how, the old Master fell off his horse and broke his neck.

Because of the weather, they buried him hurriedly. The crying of the women and the lamentations of the men were heard for several days, at the end of which, the lawyer stood at the foot of Rubén's bed, and whether he could hear it or not, he read him the will. All of those who worked in the big house were present, and those who didn't fit in the room were pressed together near the windows.

It was the Master's wish that all those who worked on the hacienda, in the house, and in the fields, would continue in the service of his son. If Rubén died, they would have to leave, and the land along with the house would pass into the hands of the church.

One morning, long after a silver strand had already appeared in Master Rubén's hair, the cane used to feed him became plugged and the liquid spilled over, running down his neck. Aunt Tomasa wiped him down with alcohol and lavender water, and while briskly rubbing his arms, she looked uneasily toward the windows. She sent Zacarías in search of Uncle Jaco.

The boy saw them put their heads together several times. Their bodies stooped down, then straightened up; they gestured with their arms and whispered things he didn't want to understand.

Aunt Tomasa told him to go to bed, that she would take care of the Master. As he was leaving, he saw the old man Jaco taking a bag out from under his clothes. The next day, Zacarías entered through the kitchen door and crossed the hall where the heads of deer and buffalo were hanging. There was even a wild turkey with its wings open on the table. With that last trophy, he thought, Jaco had really outdone himself: the turkey looked as if it were about to take off flying.

Zacarías finally arrived at the patient's room and he put the fan in motion.

He looked at the mountains in the distance and at the sky, that seemed very blue. The morning breeze brought the smell of damp earth to him. It was good to live on the hacienda, Zacarías told himself; it was good to know that he would never have to leave, because there was no doubt, he thought, looking at Master Rubén, that Uncle Jaco had done an excellent job.

Inés Fernández Moreno was born in Buenos Aires in 1947, where she grew up "feeling like a fish out of water" due to her parents' divorce when she was eight years old. Divorce was unacceptable during that time in Argentina, and Fernández Moreno recalls that she was shunned by other girls at school because of it.

Feeling unsure of herself, Fernández Moreno had several false starts in her career. She initially attempted to follow her mother's plan for her to study law at the university, but dropped out after a year because it bored her. In 1967 she was awarded a scholarship to study in Spain, where she remained for a year, traveling and hitchhiking her way across Europe. When she returned to Argentina in 1968, the country was in turmoil, and although she entered the university again, she found it in ruins; the best professors had left, students were searched before entering, and the streets outside were lined with soldiers on horseback.

Several other attempts to finish her studies followed; she pursued medicine, art, contemporary dance, and then literature, finally graduating from the University of Buenos Aires in 1975.

Feeling that there was an overabundance of writers in her family, Fernández Moreno initially shied away from writing. She began to work in public relations, and then, in 1990, it occurred to her to try writing. Fernández Moreno was greatly motivated in her efforts by a writing workshop led by Abelardo Castillo and Sylvia Iparraguirre, who gave her the final encouragement she needed.

Since that time, Fernández Moreno has won several awards for her fiction. In 1991, one of her stories, "Dios lo bendiga," was a finalist in the Concurso Juan Rulfo. In 1992, "A Mother to Be Assembled" won the Premio La Felguera in Spain and was subsequently published along with other winning stories in *Antología "Cuentos de La Felguera 1956–1993."*

In 1993, Fernández Moreno published her first book of short stories titled *La vida en la cornisa.* In 1996, her second collection of short stories, *Efectos secundarios,* was published by Emecé in Buenos Aires. Inés Fernández Moreno currently works as the creative director for a public relations firm in Buenos Aires while continuing to write fiction.

"A Mother to Be Assembled" is an autobiographical story relating a mother's attempt to provide for the needs of her children, no matter what the cost to herself. The narrator suffers from the many demands placed on the "modern woman" who attempts to be a good mother, yet cannot help but feel resentment towards her children.

A Mother to Be Assembled

by Inés Fernández Moreno

*T*he first to go were my breasts. It must have happened gradually because I can't remember exactly when it occurred. I only know that one day I looked in the mirror and they were no longer there. They had vanished completely, leaving slight pearly halos as a reminder that they had once existed.

I think it was Cecilia who ended up with them, because from the beginning, that seemed to be her privilege. She nursed until she was one and a half years old, she sucked a pacifier until she was four, and switching her from the bottle to a cup was a hard-won battle; I had to resort to all kinds of subterfuge. The others hardly questioned it. I noticed only a spark of reproach in Andrés's eyes, who had been weaned when he was barely fifteen days old, and not because I wanted it, but because the doctor had ordered it.

My eyes, on the other hand, lasted much longer, and that's even after they had been used to exhaustion. Watching to see if they were breathing during the night. Watching for diaper rash. Watching their somersaults. Watching how they dove into the pool. And later, watching over their homework, their triumphs in sports, their boy-friends and girlfriends, their clothing, always watching, twisting my head from one side to the other at an ever-increasing speed to take it all in. Even at night, when they were half-asleep, watching the turmoil of their nightmares. A thick veil started to cover my eyes, and when

Andrés took them, they were no longer any good. But he insisted and he probably needed my watchfulness more than any of the others.

My arms, so fragile when I was young, became stronger through the vigorous exercise of hugging, lifting, pushing, and separating; but after María's illness, long and exhausting, they entered a new cycle of lassitude. There were many months spent carrying her from one place in the city to another, because she would only accept going to the doctors and the clinics if I carried her in my arms. Anything, I would have done anything to cure her, and of course, she recovered. Since then, she feels herself to be the unquestionable owner of that part of my body.

However, other things were not settled so easily. There was a big fight with Pablo. Once, when I discarded his old tennis shoes, he threw a terrible tantrum and bit my right arm. The marks left by his teeth never disappeared. He considered them a sign of ownership. That arm carried his mark, and the left arm was in no way comparable. You had to be very careful with him; he always felt passed over. To have offered him the left arm would have seemed to him an unpardonable offense. Luckily, Marta, the most diplomatic of the girls, intervened. Since she wanted my legs, she subtly convinced him of the marvels of my waist: the center of the body, the meeting point of all the forces, near the navel! You fool, she told him. How do you suppose men lead women if not by the waist? Also by the shoulders, he said, lighting up, and the question was settled.

My legs, I must say without modesty, were lovely. Climbing up and down the stairs to serve them breakfast in bed and bring them their freshly-ironed clothes kept my legs firm and young for many years. Only my knees began to give out when Gabriel, the next to the last of the boys, was born. He alone finished them off, riding every day, round trip, on that gray horsey that carried him to Paris, walking, trotting, galloping, provoking endless laughter, leaving him lying at my feet, happy and exhausted.

When the first varicose vein appeared, Marta demanded my legs. It didn't matter to her that it was only up to the knees, provided she could have them right away. She studied, worked, had a thousand projects, was always in a hurry, always running. She needed legs that could keep up with her, strong and agile like mine.

My hair, along with my ears, were the domain of Paloma. Even as a child she couldn't fall asleep if she wasn't stroking my hair with one hand and pulling on my earlobe with the other. In time she adjusted to the hair on her blonde doll and to her feather pillow. On the other hand, until she had grown up, she maintained the habit of whispering all her secrets into my ear while she curled a lock of my hair around her fingers. When she left home, she took it all and left in exchange the dishevelled blonde doll that I still keep on the top shelf in my room.

I discovered that my back was missing the day it no longer hurt. I don't know which one of them could have taken it. I remembered that Juan had asked me for it so he could use it when he played with his toy cars. Stretched out on the floor, my spine was a track of perfect curves for his game. Gabriel also used it. Every time he cried, he would hug me from behind, pressing his moist cheeks against my back, following me around, stuck to me like a stamp and stumbling all over the house. Cecilia, when she wanted to get something special, would softly scratch my back until I got goose-bumps. But Francisco was the most intense. When I least expected it, he would come running full speed down the hall and jump on my back, then he would climb up to my shoulders as if he were climbing a mountain, stepping on my hips and on each one of my ribs.

I would have missed my cheeks if I had still had hands. I used to like to rest my chin on my hands and think, seated in the kitchen, when everyone was asleep, during those brief moments until one of them asked for a glass of water or woke up frightened and demanding my presence.

It's true that my cheeks had become worn by tears, and to be fair, also by kisses. But the right one disappeared suddenly the day that Javier dared to hit me, when I forbade him to go on that summer camp-out. I, myself, threw the left cheek to him as well, and not out of generosity, but out of anger. After that it was too late for demands. And that's how my face remained, a vertical line supported by my brow and by the bridge of my nose.

They took my hands finger by finger, plucking them like grapes, fighting because there were only ten of them, and the division could not be equitable. Much less so if one considers the privilege of the index finger or the tenderness of the thumb, which they fought over between piercing shrieks.

As far as my sex, which was perhaps the most thorny subject, they were intelligent children and they quickly understood that they would all need it to love and hate alternately. That is why it appeared and disappeared from my body with such frequency that I never knew when I could count on it. I preferred, then, to give it up as lost since its sudden, random disappearances kept me jumpy and fearful.

My feet were almost the last to go. I know they were wide and not very elegant, and perhaps even a little unpleasant. How silly, however, that no one valued their reliability in sustaining the difficult architecture of our family.

Pedro, the youngest, who used to dance by standing on my feet, finally took them with a contemptuous gesture, thinking he wasn't getting much. I reminded him about the story of Puss and Boots and the inheritance of the youngest of the miller's sons, which finally gave him riches and happiness. Pedro stood there thinking, then shrugged his shoulders as if it didn't matter to him and went off to live his life. Time proved that I had not been mistaken.

Of course, a multitude of minor pieces remained, which they also divided up, fighting for them to the last fiber.

But no one dared go after my voice. They knew that it was unobtainable, a possession that I could not transfer to them lest I disappear.

In recent years, when I am nothing more than a mere shadow sustained by memories, the returns have begun to arrive: perhaps a hand one day, or my waist another day.

Yesterday, for instance, my breasts arrived from Europe, where Cecilia now lives. They were magnificently preserved, full and fragrant like those of a young mother. I was so pleased that it made up for the disappointing appearance of my back, shrunken, skinny, in tatters, the vertebrae miserably worn-down as if they had lived three lives. Poor Francisco, he had always had the nefarious power of transforming every delicate object into an old rag.

I now have recovered nearly all my parts. They are stored and waiting along with Paloma's doll and all the other objects that once belonged to them. Since I am very tired, I keep putting off the final inventory. Besides, I have the nagging suspicion that something important is missing, and it isn't simply the passing of time. It's something more immaterial yet, that lingers on in all the memories from their childhood, their adolescence, their youth. Perhaps I will realize it when I begin to assemble all the parts. They have asked me to do that. They are as restless and impatient now as when they took them away. Sooner or later I will overcome this heavy lethargy. Yes, one of these days I'll make up my mind and I'll give them that last pleasure.

Born in Guayaquil, Ecuador, in 1952, Gilda Holst Molestina continues to reside in that coastal city where she studied literature at the Universidad Católica de Guayaquil. Since then she has worked in a variety of educational capacities: as a professor of Ecuadorian and Latin American literature at the Universidad Católica, as the Director of Research at the Escuela de Literatura, as the Project Director of Pedagogy, and currently as the Assistant Director of the Escuela de Literatura y Comunicación at the Universidad Católica.

Holst Molestina began to write in 1980 when she was completing her literature studies at the university, but the decision to dedicate herself to writing as a profession grew out of her participation in a writing workshop in Guayaquil, sponsored by Casa de la Cultura Ecuatoriana, Núcleo del Guayas, and coordinated by Miguel Donoso Pareja. Since that time, Holst Molestina has published numerous short stories in literary journals in Ecuador and the United States, but her work is appearing in translation here for the first time.

Although Holst Molestina willingly chose to be a writer, she feels that women writers in Ecuador encounter many obstacles. "Paternalism and maternalism, condescension, indifference, contempt, is what we face as writers. The overall situation of Ecuadorian literature is sad; there are few readers." Publishing in Ecuador, as in many Latin American countries, is extremely difficult. There is no type of government support (the preferred arts, which are sponsored, are music and theater, among others). The few opportunities there are to publish are with publishers in the capital of Quito, and authors must often pay for the publication and promotion of their work. Once work is published, there is little dissemination of it either inside or outside of Ecuador. Holst Molestina laments, "Publishing here is almost like being unpublished!"

Holst Molestina's stories are often quite brief and portray characters embroiled in conflict. Many of her protagonists are women or young girls who must deal with everyday problems which are uniquely "feminine." The protagonists of her story "The Competition" are a class of adolescents who grapple with their identity, self-confidence, gender roles, and issues of esteem as they strive to reach maturity, "mentored" by a sadistic teacher who receives great satisfaction from preying on his students' sexual insecurities. However, the teacher's cruelty is repaid many times over by one of his female victims whose chosen form of vengeance is humiliation, not so unlike what the teacher himself has done to his students.

Holst Molestina is currently preparing a collection of short stories tentatively titled *Salpico de tinta a un lector distraído* to be published by Casa de la Cultura Ecuatoriana, "Benjamín Carrión" in Guayaquil.

The Competition

by Gilda Holst Molestina

The agreement was to know the lesson and look unflinchingly (or as much as possible) at some classmate of the opposite sex while we were reciting. The deal wasn't even a verbal one; we simply began to do it when classes began during the month of August. It didn't occur to any student in particular. It came out of Dr. Muñoz's decision to introduce a new sequence in the lessons. During the first semester he had chosen a student whose last name began with an *A*, another whose name began with *Z*, and so on successively until he got to the *M*s. He always finished with Mariscal, Martínez, and Mendieta.

In August everything changed. That was the month when, for the first time, we opened our book titled *Anatomy, Physiology, and Hygiene* by R. Vidal. We assured ourselves that we'd talk with the same indifference as always. Naturally, Dr. Muñoz was missing from our conversations because he terrified us with his crudeness. According to him, he treated us the same as he did his first-year medical students at the state university. Sometimes we liked this because it made us feel important, but we cursed him with a vengeance when we had to memorize all the apophyses, fossae, and small fossae of the bones.

This month, we were finally given a scientific reason explaining why we've used deodorant for about two years. We learned that the armpit had another function besides lying beneath the arm, which was a minor function compared to the others. It was the same with the hair on our legs, the changes in our voices, the pimples on our faces, which were all symptomatic of the fiery material our bodies were made up of.

Dr. Muñoz named and quartered the human body on the blackboard with the chalk held between his thumb and index finger. Curving the other three fingers upward, he would randomly point out the body and its functions: scrotum, vulva, morula, prostate, semen, uterus. After his classes, no one would erase the board. We always waited for another professor to request it, then, while the chalk dust fell, nervous laughter would surface from different points around the classroom, while students elbowed one another.

"Señorita Martínez, describe the male sexual organs for us."

When Carla stood up, Alvarez, the first on the list, sat down, surprised. Dr. Muñoz put his hands behind him, and out of the corner of his eye, he waited for the rush of blood, which in a manner of seconds spread over her face. He walked up and down the row near Carla, and every now and then, he demanded more explanation and detail. Carla never lost her purple color, but she finished and did well. When she sat down, you could hear a sigh of relief on the part of the girls. Almost immediately, Dr. Muñoz called on Rodríguez to describe the female sexual organs, automatically creating expectations to see how it would turn out. Rodríguez was the most experienced in the class; gossip was that he had already been with prostitutes. He was a braggart and loved for others to hear him swear. Later, he would apologize to the girls, but coming from him, the apologies sounded hypocritical and offensive. He stood up, pale. He looked directly at Natalie, who had the misfortune of being crazy about him, and without taking his eyes off her, shifting his weight from one foot to another, he described the female sexual organs without interruption to the very end. All the while we saw how Natalie lowered her eyes, her head, and gradually turned red.

Dr. Muñoz stroked his stiff beard in an attempt to keep a grimace from escaping from between his teeth, which were covered by a layer of greenish plaque. Whether he realized or not what was happening, we never found out, because no one had the opportunity to ask him.

There were some parents who complained to the administration, but Muñoz laughed at them and at us in class. He told us we were a bunch of spoiled rich kids, that we were full of prejudices, and that sex, just like digestion and respiration, was a bodily function, and therefore it had to be treated scientifically. When he called on us to recite, we all said that we didn't know the information. Irritated, Muñoz warned us that if the same thing happened in the next class, we would all get a red mark in his grade book. That day he talked about nocturnal emissions, which occur frequently in adolescents, and about masturbation. Laughter and looks of guilt filled the room. Muñoz told us that it was something normal in adolescent males, but only when not abused, and in the case of females, when it happened, was abnormal. According to him, he had verified this and claimed it brought about certain consequences and future problems in married life. On that point, Sandra Castillo raised her hand and said that she had heard that masturbation in adolescents was just as normal in males as in females. Muñoz stared at her for awhile in silence.

"Where did you hear that, Señorita?"

"A priest said it," she stammered.

"Are you saying that a priest told you that?"

"Yes," Sandra answered imperceptibly.

Then Muñoz, with a raised eyebrow and a twisted smile, said slowly:

"Thank you for your opinion, Señorita Castillo. You can take your seat." And he went on to tell us office secrets about insatiable married women who had told him that when they couldn't reach climax, they manually helped themselves at the moment of their husband's climax or right after. He had begun to talk about nymphomania when the bell rang.

The whole class assumed that Sandra masturbated. More than a week passed during which she was harassed in the hallways with the words "nympho" and "masturbator." The girls continued to walk with her and speak to her as if nothing had happened, but we were too worried about appearing normal and pure to defend or support her much.

Muñoz made fun of Sandra. He called on her in every class and she would invariably respond that she didn't know the answer.

"Are you sure, Señorita Castillo? Are you sure you don't want to illuminate us with your brilliance? Masturbation is a controversial subject," Muñoz would say to her, along with other similar comments. Sandra would remain quiet or would simply say *no*.

However, our competition continued, and the truth is that the girls were losing. For the boys, it was a question of honor and manliness to pass the test, if not, they felt disgraced. The same thing happened with the girls, but our reactions were always less evident. We had all acquired defensive strategies which were considered valid: looking without seeing, fixing our eyes on a shoulder or a hand, avoiding the face. Directing our bodies, our faces, and our looks toward a classmate was very difficult for the girls, and nearly always, the recitation of the lesson finished with our eyes on the black board, on the desk, or on some part of the doctor's body.

We were already discussing the physiology involved in the sexual act when we scored a victory. Ortiz, trying to imitate Rodríguez, began the lesson by looking defiantly into Natalie's eyes, and he was nearing the end when it occurred to Natalie to wink at him. Ortiz's voice caught in his throat, he stuttered, became silent, and then lost his voice altogether. After school, Ortiz and Rodríguez came to blows.

For the last class before the exam, we asked Sandra to please learn and recite the lesson. She accepted. The remaining girls studied the material as if they were also preparing to recite it. The boys did the same and did well. Our last hope was Sandra. When Dr. Muñoz called on her, his custom was, without even looking at her, to close his notebook, put his pen in his coat, and stand up, ready to begin the class. But Sandra had already stood up, and when he saw her standing there, he couldn't help but look surprised.

"You're going to recite the lesson?" he asked.

"Yes."

"Fine. Physiology of the sexual act."

"The act of love begins…"

"Señorita, use the correct terminology," Dr. Muñoz interrupted.

"Making love is a process that begins…"

"Señorita, the correct terms are coitus, copulation, or sexual act. Choose your term and begin."

"The act of love…"

"Look, Señorita, we're in a biology class, not in a class on human relations. Are you going to recite the lesson as you should?"

"I am reciting it, Doctor."

"Look, Señorita, sit down and don't waste our time."

No one understood exactly what was happening. The only thing we knew was that Sandra wasn't going to give the lesson, and therefore we had lost. Sandra's lips were trembling and she was very pale, but her pride seemed excessive and useless to us, and we believed that she had betrayed us.

We turned a cold shoulder to her, and now that I think about it, we never spoke to her again. The day before the exam, after history class, she stood in front of the class, and without raising her voice she called us a bunch of idiots and sat down again.

The exam was the same as any other. Silence, the passing out of sheets of paper, the dictation of topics to be developed. The test seemed extremely easy to us after all we had studied. Sandra finished hers and got up to turn it in. Suddenly, and no one knows from where, she took out a pistol, and pointing it at Muñoz's unmoving head, she said: "I'm going to kill you, Dr. Muñoz."

She fired three times, blew the smoke from the end of the barrel, put the gun away, and left the class laughing, while Muñoz, still holding a piece of trembling paper between his hands, peed on himself.

María Eugenia Lorenzini studied Spanish pedagogy at the University of Chile and upon graduation worked as a teacher for eighteen years. She is currently the director of the Professional Institute E.A.T.R.I. (The American School of Translators and Interpreters) in Santiago.

Born in Santiago in 1952, Lorenzini did not begin to write until she was a college student, but claims she still lacked the discipline writing required during those years. When she was in her thirties, she felt a strong need to express what she calls "an inner search," to fill blank pages with words, to interrelate them until they formed imaginary beings and worlds. She sought to fill her imagination with these words, which she hoped would later be transferred to the imagination of her readers. Through her literary creations, she feels she is able to supplement her own realities.

Lorenzini cites several major influences in her writing: feminist literature by authors such as Simone de Beauvoir and María Luisa Bombal, Latin American writers from the "Boom" generation, and her father, Juan Lorenzini Correa, the author of the novels *Presencia de niño, Caminante*, and *En citrola a Canadá*.

Lorenzini's story "Bus Stop #46" appeared in *Sustantivo... Cuentos, Adjetivo...Premiados, Género...Mujeres*, a collection of award-winning short stories published in Chile in 1991. "I wrote this story as a reaction to the condition of women in Latin American society. These women often bear an emotional burden which forces them to live a repressed life due to the ethical and moral values placed on them by society." Lorenzini describes this society as one which recognizes three primary roles for women: mother, wife, housewife. "Women who find themselves alone, as does the protagonist in this story, who do not fulfill one of these roles, have no true identity. They live a precarious existence which makes them a target for the cruel and malicious attitudes and comments of others, especially other women, who may be fortunate enough to fulfill one of the coveted roles in Latin American society."

Lorenzini's other works include a Spanish textbook titled *Tiempo Nuevo 7* and a novel, *Después de ayer*. She is currently completing work on a novel titled *Café amargo*, and a collection of short stories titled *De pretéritos y presentes*.

Bus Stop #46

by María Eugenia Lorenzini

She anxiously awaits the sound of the bell to announce the end of the workday.

The students leave in a mad rush while she makes a serious effort to keep from being run over by the noisy human mass.

She reluctantly removes her apron and fixes her hair which has already begun to show signs of the passing years. She smiles into a small mirror, but doesn't like the grimace that is returned to her. She slams the closet door shut.

She slowly moves toward the exit. A few familiar faces that might attempt to detain her cause her to quicken her step.

From the sidewalk out front, she watches, annoyed. All the girls from the Catholic school rush out to meet young ruffians and shamelessly throw themselves into their arms and allow their bodies to be pawed in front of whomever wants to watch.

"Disgusting," she thinks. In her day she never would have behaved in such a way. Of course, she wouldn't behave that way today, either.

While she walks to the bus stop, she feels the humid air slap her face, as if trying to awaken her senses.

As usual, the line is quite long.

"I'll have to arm myself with patience," she sighs.

She places herself behind a woman who smiles at her pleasantly. She tries to look somewhere else. Nothing bothers her more than to have to talk during the trip with one of those women who attempts to tell you her life story in five minutes.

At first she doesn't see him. A strong smell of Adams Cologne, the same one as in the provocative advertisement, causes her to turn toward the man. Immediately she is able to recognize the typical features of a man in his fifties who is trying to impress young girls with his scent.

One by one the passengers climb on the bus. She sees that not a single seat will be left for her.

"I hope it doesn't fill up too much," she thinks, remembering previous experiences.

The bus moves slowly off into the evening where every so often one of the antique street lamps casts its light onto each side of the road.

Not much time passes before the windows begin to fog up from the cold outside and the large number of people inside breathing the same air. A humid heat begins to overwhelm her. She tries to open one of the windows a little, but the woman sitting next to it won't let her.

"I'm lucky to be standing after all," she tells herself.

At least she won't be so close to the oily humidity that's coming off the windows.

When a fat woman passes behind her, she feels like the other passengers are pressing her against the sides of the seats, and what's worse, she must tolerate the stench that the fat woman leaves in her wake. She therefore notes with relief that the man wearing the cologne is approaching.

"Good thing," she consoles herself. Any cheap cologne is better than the smell of the people standing near her.

Little by little the man is coming closer. With a huge breath she attempts to capture all the scents which emanate from him, which seem more like perfume to her now.

The man moves nearer. When the bus brakes, his body brushes against hers. However, she does not become aware of his presence until the bus turns the corner and all the people lean to one side and then to the other.

Now the man is behind her. She can feel his warm breath on her neck while his body completely covers her back.

She wants to move, but that body magnetizes her.

She attempts to overcome her desire and tries to move to the back of the bus. She lets go of the strap right when the bus swerves. She's afraid she'll fall like a lead weight on the passengers to her right, but a pair of strong hands on her waist holds her in place.

For a long time she can't move. She can only feel those hands, that body standing behind her, touching her gently.

Suddenly, a mixture of anxiety, shame, and desire overcomes her. She wants to flee, but a number of passengers are in the way. She makes an effort. She stretches her hand toward the bell chord, she manages to grab hold of it, and she pulls and pulls until the bus brakes at the corner.

A muffled voice, her own voice, can be heard asking the driver to wait until she gets off.

She makes her way with difficulty past the passengers and manages to get off through the entrance.

Only when she is on the sidewalk can she look toward the bus with its illuminated cargo. There, standing in front of her, is the man. For a second she thinks he will try to get off, but right then the bus begins to move again.

From far away, she manages to make out the man's hands; they are futilely trying to tell her something.

She has to walk many blocks to reach her room. Although she is exhausted, she is unable to sleep. She tosses and turns in bed, inhaling deeply, trying to recover that aroma.

During the following nights, in the middle of her dreams, he always appears, standing inside a departing bus.

Since then, each day, the students at the Catholic school look somewhat strangely at Señorita Julia who tirelessly lines up, time after time, at the bus stop waiting for bus #46.

The youngest writer included in this volume, Andrea Maturana, was born in Santiago, Chile, in 1969. Although young, Maturana is not inexperienced; she has participated in literary workshops led by well-known Chilean writers such as Pía Barros, Antonio Skármeta, and Marco Antonio de la Parra. She thus gained the necessary skills and knowledge to subsequently direct her own workshops between 1992 and 1995.

Maturana has received a number of awards for her writing, including honorable mentions in three short story competitions in Chile, and second place in *El Concurso Encuentro Nacional de Arte* in the short story category in 1990. Her short stories have been published in over ten anthologies since 1986, including *El cuento feminista latinoamericano* (1988), *Brevísima relación del cuento breve en Chile* (1989), *Santiago, pena capital* (1991), and *Nuevos cuentos eróticos* (1991).

In Maturana's stories, the reader is allowed glimpses of everyday life, descriptions of the obvious, which often turn out to be not so obvious after all. Her writing is deeply feminine, original, and surprising. In few words, for the majority of her stories are quite brief, Maturana deftly paints, with minimalist strokes, a full and complete picture, leaving little unsaid.

Maturana's stories "Cradle Song" and "Out of Silence," powerfully exemplify her mastery of the short story. In "Cradle Song" Maturana skillfully and unforgettably presents stark and disturbing images of the poverty and suffering so common in many Latin American countries. In "Out of Silence," the narrator speaks to a painted image which haunts her from another world.

In 1992 Maturana published her first collection of short stories titled *(Des) Encuentros (Des) Esperados*. She is currently at work on a novel, which will be published under the auspices of El Fondo de Desarrollo de la Cultura y de las Artes in Chile.

Cradle Song

by Andrea Maturana

She's been reclining in the same spot for several days now. Marco, seated a few steps away from her, looks at her and supposes that she's cold. He guesses this because of her curled-up position on those uncomfortable stones cradling her bones, which little by little appear closer to the skin, every day reflecting more of herself.

He's been watching her day and night without moving, denying the hunger he feels, the cold, and the stones nearly embedded in his skin.

When he was a child, he also watched her sleep, respecting her dreams, prolonging them, wishing that he could rest while at the same time yearning to be once again the little boy she held in her arms, so he could squeeze her almost childlike breasts for that tasteless milk made of bread and water.

Now, he again savors that taste and would like her to console him, to defend him like she did before, from the rats which come to life at that hour, when the sun sets over the banks of the river. He wants to hear her say again, now Marco, go to sleep my son, sleep, little one, so you can forget your hunger for awhile, offering him the soothing pleasure of her already empty breasts.

But she doesn't understand him and she continues to sleep without noticing the rats sniffing her, flirting with her, speaking to her.

Then he stands up, feeling the marks from the stones on his legs, and he walks toward her and lifts her without difficulty, since the only thing that has any weight now is her memory. Only at that moment does he feel the pain and forgive her, embrace her, and cry without caring about the smell she emits, because what he owes her is so great. And he says to her, now, Mamita, now, the rats are leaving, you won't be hungry any more, now you will be able to rest; yes, you will.

Out of Silence

by Andrea Maturana

Afternoon is approaching, and as usual in these meetings with you, you are hidden, barely visible behind the fan. I have asked myself if your mouth is smiling, or—if I ever have the opportunity to see it—will it appear with two enormous fangs and a thin trickle of blood in the corners of your mouth. In spite of these thoughts, I have never found you to be cruel. No matter how much everyone insists, I do not see any indication of evilness or bitterness in your eyes, only wrinkles, which rather than making you unattractive, make you look more like a mother.

Do you remember that several times I offered to open the window for you?

Of course you remember. You averted your eyes and blinked negatively, and I knew you didn't want me to. You would never want a breeze to blow on you because that would eliminate the reasons for fanning yourself. In reality, saying that you fan yourself is not entirely true. Rather, you keep your hand still, covering your face, and you see how the ghosts in this house, this house I have tried to leave many times, stroll at my side.

I'm not going to leave, am I? I know you don't want me to leave and that's why you come and keep me company, although the room is filled with debris...filled with objects that everyone collected and that, one death after another (because I won't deny to you that this house has brought nothing but absences) I have been incapable of throwing away.

More than once I have tried to explain to you why I keep all of this. Not that you have asked me directly. You never ask anything directly. Discretion, of course. Perhaps it is selfish of me, because in reality, it's not for your sake that I wish to explain it, but rather to speak it aloud so that I myself can understand it. And I haven't been able to. I haven't been able to because I'm incapable of putting it into words.

Once again it has gotten late. Shadows are barely distinguishable in this place, and therefore, in the half light, I am even more intrigued by what is hidden behind the fan. Today I can no longer continue, illuminated by the candles, the colors are muted.

But today I confess to you, once and for all, and beg you to forget it, that I put that fan there on purpose. From the beginning I painted it on you, clinging onto your hand, out of the simple fear of having painted death itself on this canvas, and being forced to see your face.

Viviana Mellet initially planned to study sociology when she entered the Universidad Católica del Perú, but quickly changed to the study of literature. Ultimately, she did not finish, choosing instead to go to work. Her serious interest in writing began in 1984 when she entered a writing contest organized by Flora Tristán, a women's organization in Lima, and was awarded an honorable mention for her story. In 1991, she again entered the contest, this time with her story "Good Night Air," which was subsequently published in La tentación de escribir in Lima in 1993, as one of the winning entries of the Second Short Story Contest "Magda Portal." Viviana Mellet has since won a number of other writing awards: most recently her book of short stories titled La mujer alada won second place in a contest sponsored by Radio Sol Armonía and La Librería Studium. This honor motivated her to present her book to the publishing house Peisa, which published it in 1995.

The two stories included here, "Good Night Air," and "The Other Mariana," come from her collection *La mujer alada.* Although both are completely fictitious, "The Other Mariana" is based on Mellet's observations of life in the neighborhoods where she grew up in Lima. With this story she touches upon the themes of social ascension through marriage as well as the existence of machismo, which she feels is encouraged by women themselves. These are women who allow men to think that they alone are responsible for the economic well-being of their families, which ultimately determines their success or failure as men.

In "Good Night Air," Mellet paints a dismal portrait of a family in decline. A manipulative mother controls her son through his feelings of guilt, making him believe that he is not the son or the husband he should be. He allows his wife to stoically care for his mother, enduring the woman's hatred and abuse because it is the lot she accepted, and what was expected of her when she married.

Viviana Mellet currently works as an administrator for the Scientific Network of Peru and continues to write short fiction.

Good Night Air

by Viviana Mellet

The man opened the door carefully and entered his house. In the darkness, the colored lights projected by the television set danced on the wall of the entryway. His wife, engulfed by the sofa, was watching the eight o'clock soap opera. With the volume on low, the set was emitting an uneven buzz. The man approached with slow steps. He cleared his throat. She lifted her head and their lips brushed.

"How are you?" he asked. They both knew it wasn't necessary to answer.

"There…" his wife answered distractedly.

"And my mother?"

He didn't expect an answer for this question, either. It was the ritual that permitted him to take those five steps each night toward the door and immerse himself in the darkness of the hallway.

No, he didn't expect an answer. At one time, he had had the hope that a miracle might occur, that his wife might give an answer like, "Your mother went out to take a walk," or, "she's already asleep," or, "she's eating," or, why not admit it, she might say with the same indifferent tone, sunk on the sofa with the remote control in her hand, "she died this afternoon."

He would have been sad. He would have taken off his glasses to dry his tears. Perhaps his wife would have consoled him with a brotherly caress. But, deep down, he would have been relieved. He had lost all hope a long time ago. His mother's longevity had surpassed all reasonable limits, and he had become accustomed to the idea that time was standing still, that his life had neither a past nor a future. It consisted solely of a circular dimension that began and ended in that threshold where, before allowing himself to be enveloped by the darkness, he heard his wife repeat "there…"

He moved forward, loosened his tie, and noiselessly approached the beam of light coming from the half-closed door. Lying on the bed, his mother was watching the same soap opera as his wife, but with the volume turned up several decibels higher.

"Mami?" He lowered the volume without her noticing. The bronze chandelier brightly illuminated the room. The bedroom was spacious, with a large window facing an overgrown garden. The room was, without a doubt, the best in the house. However, filled as it was with furniture, out of date decor and having little ventilation, there was an oppressive feeling of closeness. At her age, the old woman had acquired, among other things, the habit of collecting knickknacks, and she was afraid of air currents. She exhaled a rancid breath that smelled like rotten apples.

She made an attempt to sit up, emitting a groan. Her look of helplessness traversed the room and settled like a lead weight on her son. He approached her, stooped over and dragging his feet. He kissed her on the forehead and formed the same empty and inevitable question.

"How are you?" he asked, since there was no longer any escape. The greeting was the trigger that set the circle into motion, causing it to begin to spin in the same unavoidable direction. The answer changed disguises every night, but it was always the same painful thorn which plunged itself between his kidneys.

"The same…" she said with her weak voice. "How else could a sick old woman like me be…in the way, bored, fed up."

The man pretended not to hear her. He bent over, picked some pieces of toilet paper off the floor, and threw them into the bedpan under the bed.

"You're late," the old woman scolded him.

"A lot of work," he excused himself, mumbling.

He took off his jacket and carefully placed it on the back of a chair. He sighed before asking again.

"Did you eat?"

"It's disgusting…" she sputtered.

He saw the tray sitting on the dresser with the food intact, and he moved it closer to the bed. He dipped the spoon into the soup and offered it to her, without much hope.

"You have to eat, Mama, please."

She pressed her lips together and turned her head away.

"It'll be cold," she protested.

The man took a sip and confirmed that the soup was cold.

"She brought it to me early," she grumbled, and with a contemptuous gesture she nodded toward the door. "Like a baby," she added with disgust. "I have no appetite at that time of day."

The man removed the tray and placed it back on the dresser.

"And all because she had to see to that man."

"What man?" he asked, and then realized, too late, that he had again fallen into the trap.

"Who do you suppose it was?"

"It was probably Pablo, Mama."

"I don't know…I don't think so. Your son hasn't come around here for a long time. Besides, he would have come in to say hello to his grandmother, don't you think?"

The man didn't respond. With his back to her, he put the medicine bottles and boxes in order on top of the nightstand. The old woman continued talking through her teeth.

"I didn't recognize his voice. They were talking so softly…or maybe it's because I'm going deaf."

For a moment, all that could be heard was a dripping in the bathroom. Immediately the buzzing of the television resumed.

"Come on, Mama, eat something."

"No, I don't want to."

"Even if it's only jello. I'll feed it to you."

The man arranged the pillows behind her back and smoothed the yellowed sheets. Then, bending over, he grabbed his mother by the armpits to sit her up.

"Ow, ow," she complained.

"What happened? Did I hurt you?"

She didn't answer.

"Where does it hurt?" he insisted, without losing his calm.

"Here," she said, and pointing to her hip as she asked shyly, "Will you rub it with ointment?"

He pulled up the flannel nightgown and the naked body of the woman was revealed. It was slight and pale. Her skin, thin and dry, formed folds over her abdomen, which sank into the protruding bones of her pelvis.

Her breasts hung to each side and could easily have been confused with the folds of skin on her stomach if not for the bluish shadow of the veins and the pinkish aureoles, into which her nipples sank, childlike and withered.

Her sparse white pubic hair showed her pubis, disproportionately meaty, like that of a child. She covered herself with the corner of the sheet, in a futile gesture of modesty. But the man was used to her nakedness.

"What happened?" he exclaimed when he saw her bruised hip. "Look what you've done to yourself!" he reprimanded her. "Why did you get up, Mama?"

She remained silent, sulking, with her eyes fixed on the television. The actress was crying now, with dry eyes and without ruining her makeup.

"Answer me, Mama," he raised his voice, beginning to lose control.

"Don't make me talk," she threatened.

Secretly, the man was afraid. Did he wish for something terrible to happen? For his wife to go crazy and beat the old woman, or for her to torment her, or torture her like in the movies with Bette Davis or that Crawford woman? He suspected, in spite of the horror, that the world would acquire some coherence, or that his life might take on some kind of meaning.

However, his mother's accusations always obeyed a silent bitterness whose foundation weakened with time. As the spouse of the only son, his wife attended to her mother-in-law with resignation. Without affection, but also without hatred. He was sure of that.

"Tell me," he tried to persuade her, recovering his patient tone. "What happened?"

"I wanted to see."

"What?"

"You don't believe me, son," she whined. "You don't want to see it." Her voice broke. She was sobbing. The old woman's crying became confused with the television actress's, and the sobs of the two women, dry and excessive, excised the thorn from between his kidneys.

While the man applied the ointment, he could hear his wife closing the door behind her. He thought of her hips, rounded by maturity, but still tempting. Her waist was thin, as was fashionable in the 50s, and her hair was pulled back on the nape of her neck.

With her back turned, always with her back turned. For so many years she had surrounded herself with silence and shadows, living with her back turned toward him. That night, like previous nights, he would enter the bedroom and would watch her sleeping. Was she really asleep? Her shape, outlined under the blankets, with her back turned toward him. And although this wasn't a metaphor and he had almost forgotten her face, she had never complained nor reproached him for anything. She had loved him the way he was when they had met many years ago, frugal and weak of character. But even though they had never dreamed of a perfect life, or even a passionate one, they had never imagined that they would turn into the strangers that they were now. He told himself, one more time, that he felt defeated. That in spite of his efforts, he had not managed to achieve the simple goals that he had outlined for his life: to be a good son, a good husband, a good father. He didn't know for whom, but he felt great rage.

"You never loved her, did you Mama?" he heard himself say in a sudden attack. His voice sounded like an echo, like the voice of a stranger, and he was aware that his words sounded like a reproach. He was immediately sorry, and he cowered as if trying to avoid an invisible blow. It was impossible to call back his words which floated like dust in the air. An icy silence permeated the room and his mother's eyes were fiercely riveted on his. He lowered his eyes.

"Damn her," she said slowly, enjoying every syllable. "She stole my son from me, my only son. She stole my grandchild from me." The man continued to look at the floor in silence. "She stole my things from me, my house, and imprisoned me in this room. How can I love her?"

He didn't speak. He had learned that silence, like time, healed all wounds. After a few moments, he raised his eyes and rested them on the television set while several long and viscous minutes passed. He was anxious to leave so he could go to bed, but he couldn't find an opportune moment. He was so tired. He thought he was nearly as old as his mother when he began to care for her, that he no longer had the strength to continue living. A long time passed before he decided to get up. He pretended to yawn.

"I'm dead tired," he finally said.

"I need to urinate," the old woman mumbled.

He gave her the bedpan and turned away. Then, he removed it and headed for the bathroom. From there he could hear her speaking to him.

"Don't forget that you are going to prepare my breakfast tomorrow. That woman puts tons of sugar in the coffee…"

"Yes, Mama."

"And leave enough time so you can join me."

"Yes, Mama."

"Don't forget to put a clean bedpan for me next to the bed."

"Uh-huh," he answered docilely. And without making any noise, he placed the bedpan next to the toilet and washed his hands.

He returned to the bedroom and turned off the light and the television set.

"Make sure the window is closed tight, will you?" she said in a weak voice. She had closed her eyes and her gray hair shone in the dark. "I don't want one of those drafts to kill me."

"Yes, Mami," he answered. He approached the bed, and bending over, kissed his mother on the forehead. "Good night, Mama," he said.

Then, before his silhouette moved down the hallway, stooped and dragging its feet, he approached the window and opened it wide.

The Other Mariana

by Viviana Mellet

*T*he light. Ernesto gets up to turn it on. This time of day always makes him nervous. The sky turns pale and the clouds seem to be in a hurry, like the people on the street who run to catch the bus. The fluorescent lights flicker before lighting up the office while Ernesto returns to his desk. He finishes jotting down numbers on a slip of paper which he folds and deposits in a drawer. He then puts some papers in order, places his appointment book in the drawer, puts on his jacket, and leaves.

In the building's lobby the doorman is having coffee and donuts. It got late on me, Ernesto tells him, tipping his hat in a gesture of good-bye. The doorman responds by shrugging his shoulders. He'll have to take a taxi, there's no other choice at this time of day since he doesn't have the car. He's not accustomed to walking around downtown. He normally comes in and leaves by car. He knows how to take care of himself in traffic, but while walking he runs into people, he steps on merchandise for sale on the sidewalk, he brushes against the dirty walls.

He stops the first unoccupied taxi he sees in the confusion of cars and the din of honking horns. He climbs in like a man grabbing for a life vest. Once inside, he realizes that it's an old and dilapidated car, with seats covered with stained and dirty upholstery. It smells like fish, and the driver seems to be one of those guys who likes to talk politics. Ernesto has no desire to talk, but while the car heads toward the boulevard, he feels a great relief, almost joy. He's heading toward home. The air entering through the broken window blows through his hair and carries away the fishy odor as downtown begins to fall behind. The mildewed buildings and the crowds also disappear behind them as evening begins to descend over the trees lining the street. He suddenly realizes that the driver has not taken the express-way. Too late! He's a talker and he doesn't care if he's delayed by stoplights every two blocks; this is more likely a pleasant pretext for prolonging the conversation. The driver is telling him a new version of the latest scandal, one Ernesto had already heard at lunchtime: there is a new terrorist group which seems to have come from the far right. Ernesto responds with monosyllables. He's thinking only about getting home, jumping in the shower, and drinking a whisky on the rocks in the darkness of his living room. Today was a day from hell. It's Wednesday and all he wants to do is sit in the dark and watch a movie. The driver insists that the new terrorist group is the result of the police's low salaries, making them resentful of the government. Ernesto agrees, some movie with lots of scenery, lots of green and blue; a blonde like Ursula Andress or Bo Derek, on a tropical island or somewhere like that. Yeah…exactly, the cops are poorly paid. The driver warms up to the subject because something is blocking traffic, a huge bus stopped sideways in the road. And now, with the car motionless, the driver can speculate at will about what the Minister of the Interior will say tonight on television.

That's when Ernesto sees her. "Mariana!" he thinks. Standing underneath the green light of a neon sign, her paleness is accentuated, giving her a ghostlike quality. Besides, she *is* ghostlike, an apparition, because she's like Mariana's negative. Identical, but opposite. What in Mariana is slenderness, in this woman is weakness; what in Mariana is vivacity, in the other woman is nervousness; what in one is an attribute, in the other is an imperfection. The taxi remains stopped. Ernesto pays. I'll get out here, he says, without waiting for his change. If it weren't for the fact that he *knows* that at this moment Mariana is activating the remote control, the garage door is slowly opening, the tires on the Jaguar are crushing the gravel of the driveway like cellophane, he would swear that she led a double life.

You have a double, he would tell her later, exactly like you, walking down other streets, living a life in exactly the opposite direction as yours. But he knows that Mariana is returning from the art opening in Chichi, happy with her new Márquez painting. He follows her, captivated by the amazing similarities and by the abysmal differences. He feels that he has entered another dimension of time and space, and that he, also, has been split in two, and that the man who is walking behind the woman is no longer obeying his will.

Her hair rains down over her shoulders—opaque, no cream rinse, no dyes, no tortoiseshell barrette—this caricature of Mariana who frees the brake on a rusty baby stroller and pushes it with one hand. Her other hand is holding a bag filled with bread rolls. A child standing near her grabs on to her skirt, crying. Up, he demands. She looks at him uneasily and says something to him that Ernesto is unable to hear. He is about ten feet away and has begun to follow her, knowing that what he's doing is absurd, but that he'll do it anyway. The woman turns into a dark alley. Some street kids are playing ball. The ball rolls in front of the child, who transforms his whimpering into outright sobbing and refuses to walk any further. Mariana's hand—without the Cartier rings made of burnished silver and gold, without Russian diamonds— lets go of the stroller to console the crying child with a caress. The stroller begins to roll down the sidewalk. She reaches it and stops it abruptly. Now the baby inside the stroller is crying too. Three bread rolls have fallen from the bag and landed in a puddle. Mariana—who is not accustomed to dealing with children, because that is what nannies are for—becomes impatient, threatens a spanking, raises her voice, but ends up lifting the child. She begins to walk, pushing the stroller with her leg. Mariana's leg, which she forgot to wax, which she doesn't wax, which she shaves with her husband's razor. Ernesto imagines the roughness of the other Mariana's calves, the other Mariana who turns the corner maneuvering the stroller. The child's tears and snot slide down her curved shoulder. It has already become dark, but Ernesto continues to feel dusk's departure. Through the windows that face the street he sees that televisions are on in dining rooms. Families are eating in silence, absorbed in the Minister of the Interior's words. But this Mariana, surely, has run out of gas for the stove, and tonight for dinner she'll serve bread and avocados and coffee with milk. She's tired and desperate because the two children are crying at the same time, and she still has to go and boil water at her neighbor's house.

At home, Mariana has turned on the radio—today there's a jazz program. She's smoking a cigarette, and while sprawled on the sofa, she decides that it's time to reupholster the chaise lounge. Perhaps something oriental with some Hawaiian palms behind it…and on the wall, the new Márquez…. Oh no, better yet, a fruit salad, and standing next to the fruit cart, her dirty sandals step on some banana peels. And Ernesto is surprised by how much he has of Mariana, his Mariana, the one without his protection, his love, and all his prosperity.

How common and pitiful is the weariness of this woman. But why does Ernesto feel a bitter tenderness when he watches her? The risk was eliminated from Mariana's life at the precise moment she swore *till death do us part.* Then he offered her everything, because a woman like that *deserves the best in the world.* What does this crude imitation of Mariana deserve? Could he possibly approach her and lend her a hand? Could he remove her from this dimension as if he were erasing her from a drawing and recover the Mariana from a time when everything still remained a possibility? Bury his face in her warm neck and swear to her, I'm going to make you happy, Mariana, I'm going to give you everything you deserve, you'll have whatever you desire. But please, don't alter your expression, don't form that scornful sneer with your lips, don't ever again make that face indicating bored satisfaction.

I'll cross the street, thinks Ernesto, while the woman is choosing some oranges. I'll turn my back to her and I will no longer look at this sad parody of Mariana. It's a question of only five or six blocks and he will be walking down the tree-lined streets of his neighborhood, arriving at his house, feeling the crunch of gravel beneath his feet, and then the lushness of the carpet. Mariana will smugly show him her new Márquez, and she'll announce that a peach-colored brocade would be perfect for the chaise lounge. And wrapped in his plush robe, with a glass in his hand and the ice cubes tinkling, Ernesto will tell her, you have a double, Mariana, near here, on the other side of the park. She'll look at him out of the corner of her eye, an expression that says *who in this neighborhood could look like me, please, Ernesto.* A woman in sandals, burdened with packages, whose moist shoulder Ernesto now wishes to touch, to rescue her from her bleak existence, and perhaps recover an expression.

But Mariana is looking at him, from deep inside the story

imprisoning her. She's looking at him with that reproachful expression, and she's saying to him what are you doing standing there, come and help with the bags; there's no gas, damn it, and when will you get it refilled? Take these, will you, she's telling him, bad humored, as usual. "I can't carry all of this. Oh, and I should warn you: there's not a drop of water."

Ana María Shua has worked as a professor, journalist, and screen writer, and has published numerous works in a variety of genres. Her creative works include theatrical presentations, collections of poetry, short stories, novels, children's books, and collections of essays. One of her novels, Los amores de Laurita, was made into a movie of the same title in 1986 in Argentina. Shua also wrote the screenplay for this work.

Born in Buenos Aires in 1951 into a Jewish family, Shua claims that "Jewishness" is a very important element in her writing and is always present in some way in her work. Many of her characters and some of the themes she deals with in her works are what Shua calls "naturally Jewish," without having to declare it or justify it.

Her novel, *El libro de los recuerdos,* published in 1994, traces the history of a Jewish family that immigrated to Argentina. Readers are introduced to the immigrant grandparents, to their children who become merchants in Buenos Aires, and finally, to the grandchildren who struggle to keep their lives together in a changing society.

Many of Ana María Shua's works also show a marked satirical and black sense of humor. Her story, "A Profession Like Any Other," is a grotesque parody of the power wielded by a sadistic dentist over a helpless patient. Some critics have suggested that the story is a metaphor for the era of the "dirty wars" in Argentina when the dictatorship blatantly abused its citizens' human rights. Shua denies this was her conscious intention when she wrote the story. "If I had thought during that time that the story could have had anything to do with the dictatorship, I would not have written it because I was very afraid." She does not rule out, however, the subconscious effect that this difficult period in Argentina's history may have had on her creative production. "Viewing it now from a distance, it's possible that it had something to do with that process."

"Minor Surgery" is a semi-autobiographical story, about which Shua says: "I began to write the story believing that it would be easy to relate my own experience of abortion, which turned out to be impossible, because, among other reasons, when I had the procedure done, my father and my boyfriend were in the waiting room while my mother was with me, holding my hand."

Ana María Shua's works have recently been receiving a great deal of notice outside of Argentina. Many of her short stories have been translated into other languages and included in anthologies published in Canada, the United States, Italy, Holland, Spain, Mexico, and England. Two of her three novels, *El libro de los recuerdos* and *Los amores de Laurita*, are being translated into English for publication in the United States. Her third novel, *Soy paciente (Patient)*, is scheduled for release in English this year by Latin American Literary Review Press.

A Profession Like Any Other

by Ana María Shua

"*S*it still, will you? There we go, hmmm, that's a really deep cavity. I don't like this at all. No, no, don't close your mouth yet, I'm going to start the suction. I hope I don't have to do a root canal, but I don't know, let's take a look. Easy, easy, there, that's good. How's your cousin Enrique? That guy really had a mess of a mouth. By the way, you know he only paid half of what he owes me? I knew it. I had a hunch…Don't move now. Look, it's going to be a little difficult to work on that molar from this angle. I'll have to go through your ear to reach it. I'll need to perforate the eardrum, but don't worry, I'll give you a little local anaesthesia and you won't feel a thing. Just a little prick. That's right, don't move because if the scalpel slips it could cost you your brain. As I was saying, one becomes a bit of a practicing psychologist in this business. You can tell by a person's face if they're going to stiff you. If he weren't a cousin of yours, I never would have given that guy credit. That's right, I would have had him pay me in advance or I wouldn't have worked on him. It's not only the hours of work that you lose, but do you know what these materials cost? Everything's imported. You can get products made here, but they're not the same. A responsible dentist likes to work with the best. Look, let's suppose that if after I perforate your eardrum and I manage to put in a filling, it falls out after two months. Then the cavity gets deeper; you wouldn't come back, and you'd be absolutely right not to.

Careful, please. There it is. The anaesthesia is working great, but you'll probably still feel a little pain, you can't avoid it. Let's see, let's do this. When it really hurts, raise your hand and I'll stop, okay? Today the salesman came in with some drill bits for the ultrasonic drill...a real wonder. Everyday they invent something new. But the cost! Don't you believe it, the drills wear out, too. Everything wears out and then you have to fix it. Anyway, let's don't even talk about repair costs. Okay, okay, I'll stop. Can you hear anything from your right ear? No, don't try to talk because if you close your mouth you'll ruin all my work. Answer me by nodding your head. No, of course not, you don't hear anything. Well, it doesn't matter. You'll probably never hear from that ear again, but you won't feel any pain in that molar either, and that's what's important. Isn't that right? You were right to come in now before it got too bad. Imagine, there are people who only remember to go to the dentist when they can't sleep at night because they're in so much pain. They end up in here with all kinds of inflammation and then nothing can be done. You have to go to the dentist regularly, at least every six months if you have a problem mouth. If not, then once a year, even if nothing is bothering you. Well, we've finished with this. Rinse and spit and get ready because now comes the hard part. We're going to take an x ray. Close your mouth for me for a second. There, very good. We'll have it developed for your next visit. Oh, but this bicuspid is a real shame. Who put this filling in? No, don't close yet. A white filling. Sure, something new comes out, and there are those dentists who immediately want to use it for everything. That can't be. You have to be really careful with new things; you have to test them little by little. See, for example, to take this white filling out, I'm going to have to remove your eyeball. Don't worry because afterwards I'll put it back in, and it'll be just like new. How awful, huh, I don't like the way your mouth looks at all. On the other side you have another filling just like it, white, too. What a disaster. I don't want to criticize my colleagues, but there are all kinds of irresponsible types out there, you know? That's what you get for going to the competition. No, I meant it as a joke. Well, it won't be necessary to put you out completely. Still, it's going to seem like everything gets dark when I take the eyeball out, but you won't feel any pain. I'll put these drops on your eyelids, and the anesthesia will penetrate immediately. Just another little prick right here and that's it.

You aren't going to believe me, but the bigger they are, the more afraid they are of the dentist. Sometimes it's easier to work with little children than grown men. When I was doing my residency at Argerich, I almost always got the dock workers, as big as houses, used to moving cargo, but as soon as they saw the needle they fainted. You, on the other hand, are behaving very well. I congratulate you for being so brave. Now you're going to act as my helper so you'll forget about what's happening and won't get so tense. Try to relax more. All set? Good, here it is, with your right hand you hold on to this eyeball while I take out the other one. Don't squeeze it or the lens will pop out. A little eyeball with the retina, see? Perfect. One day one of those patients from the hospital came to my private office. A longshoreman, I think. I was, pardon the expression, scared shitless. I mean, if I hurt this guy, the first thing he'd have done is give me a black eye. What happened was that just watching me prepare the drill the guy up and died on me. What a mess with the guy there dead in the chair. It had to have been a heart attack. Well, one of the occupational hazards, don't you think? Anyway, you were lucky with this tooth. If you had waited a little longer, we wouldn't have been able to save it. But this other one, that one isn't too bad. It's because those white fillings are a curse, see? It's one of those things where what's good about it is also bad. It's so hard that you can't get through it. It's extremely hard. Sure, but if they don't put a good base underneath to insulate it, what happens? The cavity keeps growing underneath the filling and to get rid of it, I tell you, is no joke. You'll feel how hard I have to work at it. That's for sure. I always use a base. It takes a little longer, and the patient has to come in two or three times, but when it's finished, it's finished right and I'm sure there won't be any more problems. That's it. For now I'll leave it like that. Now, rinse and spit. We'll make an appointment for next week. Is Thursday at seven thirty all right? Answer me by nodding your head so you can get used to doing that, because I had to cut off the tip of your tongue and at first people will have trouble understanding you. You didn't even feel it, right? You see how great the anaesthesia is? But don't worry, with a good speech therapist you'll get along fine. Your diction will probably be a little strange, but hey, since you're not an actor or a newscaster…It's marvelous the things they can do nowadays in that area. To think that just a hundred years ago those things didn't even exist. Well, Thurs-

day at seven thirty, then. Meanwhile, I'll put those eyes of yours in
formaldehyde so they keep, and next time when you come in, or the
time after that, I'll put them back in. Of course, you won't be able to
see, but they'll be just fine, and no one will ever know that they had
been taken out. That's right, I put in a base that's really good, but it
hasn't set yet, so don't be eating anything from now till Thursday or
you'll ruin all my work, okay? Oh yes, and give my best to your cousin
Enrique."

Minor Surgery

by Ana María Shua

*I*t's a house just like all the others on the block: a good house built in the 30s. It has two entrances and two stone gargoyles above each, but you have to look up to discover them. You have to be very attentive to notice all the details, the moldings, the finish of the wooden door. You have to imagine the stained-glass windows that open onto the patio, in order to keep from looking at all the women who are standing in the street under a light rain.

There are a lot of them; there are also a few men. It's difficult to count them exactly while carefully trying to avert your eyes. It's better to look at their faces, and not their bellies. But it's impossible not to stare at the bellies of the other women who now enter the house, urged on by a nurse who intermittently sticks her head out the door and calls them with energetic gestures: come on, come on, you can't stay in the street.

And although Gerardo goes in with her, from that moment on, Laura is alone. Inside there are more women and a few men, and they all crowd together in a small central room with three old, gray plastic chairs with metal armrests, and a dusty library with decorations that seem to subtly allude to the peculiar profession of its owner. A family of grotesque porcelain elephants, a group of Russian dolls that fit inside one another, a bas-relief of the Heart of Jesus (the long-haired, open-thorax version, where Jesus stands alongside his disembodied heart, surrounded by twig-like shapes which are supposed to represent rays of divine illumination); and, in a picture frame, a photograph of three identical baby girls, triplets, at the beach, wearing little buttoned hats and pleated bathing suits. It's obvious that they hate being there, facing the sun, squinting their eyes to protect them from the glare. They look as if they're about to cry at any moment; the photographer will have to click quickly. He will have to finish in a hurry.

One by one, called in order of their arrival, the women enter the examining room with their companions and leave immediately, with a little piece of green paper in their hands, to continue their wait.

Laura and Gerardo enter the examining room without holding hands. The doctor is a large, fat man, dressed in a very clean white uniform. He's talking on the telephone, demanding that they send him those samples right away. They're the tiles that he plans to install in the sun room of his weekend house; he'll explain later, he says, excusing himself. And he spends a few minutes describing the house that he and his family enjoy from September through April and why not, in winter as well. It's always good to get out of the city, to breathe some fresh air.

The doctor looks like the prosperous owner of a restaurant. It's possible to imagine him controlling the activities of his employees, the hunks of cooked ham that fall one by one onto the wax paper, opening the oven where the chickens slowly rotate so he can turn them one more time with his expert finishing touch.

Laura can't take her eyes off his hands, those small fat hands that are going to work on her body. The doctor is reduced to a one-dimensional image of his hands moving efficiently, accepting the money, giving Laura a number that he tears off a green receipt book. It's number eleven, but don't worry, I'll call you early, the doctor assures them, speaking as if he were their friend.

And it's true, barely half an hour of waiting has passed when they call Laura by her name, in spite of the slip of paper that shows the number eleven. They call her in fifth place; the doctor has fulfilled his promise; she'll be one of the first. However, after drinking the black perfumed wine from his vessel, the favor that the Cyclops has bestowed upon Ulysses in the name of hospitality is that he agrees to eat him last, after all his companions. But Laura rejects the comparison. She doesn't plan to thrust a sharp stake through the doctor's eye, because she also feels partially grateful, and besides, the doctor isn't a cyclops, the other eye will always remain with him.

She enters another room guided by the nurse. Surely this room was one of the bedrooms in the house's original floor plan, separated by a hallway from the examining room facing the front. Off to one side there's a screen; they have her undress there and put on a blue hospital gown, mended and clean, highly starched. There are two twin beds. Seated on one of them is a woman with long hair and an expressionless face. She's barefoot and in her slip, but has already put back on her skirt. The other bed holds another woman, still half-asleep. She's moaning and turning and twisting, thrashing her legs. She's wearing a gown, which because of her movements, has come open, and you can see her bloody thighs and between her legs (but not much). The pad that has slipped from its place when she opened her legs is replaced by the nurse who wakes her up with little energetic and affectionate slaps given with the back of her hand on the patient's cheeks. The woman opens her eyes, closes her legs, and shuts up.

The doctor's assistant carries in another woman who is wearing a gown and is half-asleep. The man is tall and strong, but he can barely lift the weight of the woman. He would need help if the patient were fatter or bigger. He carefully deposits her on the bed where the woman with long hair is seated in her slip. She gets up to make room for the newcomer, moving over to sit in a chair.

Now a girl who is almost as young as Laura and who already has her gown on has her turn. Laura expects them to call her by using the traditional "who's next, the next one should come on in," but it isn't like that. The doctor leaves the examining room, he approaches the young girl, and taking her by the hand he leads her to the farthest corner from the door. Now, prepare yourself for a little race, he tells her, one, two, three, and hop, and run, and the two of them trot, holding hands, into the examining room. The assistant also enters and closes the door.

Laura is unable to comprehend the meaning of this small additional humiliation. It must be for the hysterical ones, the woman with the long hair tells her, who is now putting on her sweater, shoes, looking for her purse; it's for the girls who change their minds at the last minute and begin to scream.

But none of the women there seem about to have an attack of hysteria, much less about to change their minds. The woman who is no longer moaning is seated on the bed and is beginning to put on her underwear, her stockings, which the nurse hands to her. All the employees' movements are synchronized; they've managed to organize an efficient assembly line allowing them to run through fifteen cases in one morning.

After about ten or fifteen minutes, the woman with the long hair will leave and the one who is no longer moaning will take her place on the bed. The assistant will carry in the other girl and it will be Laura's turn. She decides to use that time to make up a dignified and well-constructed sentence, a sentence that should be said in a calm tone of voice and slightly ironically so the doctor will allow her to enter the examining room walking normally, avoiding the one, two, three, hop, the little race, since that's the only thing she can avoid now.

But when the doctor arrives to take her by the hand, Laura's mouth is dry and the ingenious words don't come out. Everything happens quickly, there's no time to resist, one, two, three, hop, a little race, and Laura would already be lying on the table with her legs raised and supported by two metal stirrups if she had not pulled away suddenly with a brusque movement that came from within, away from the doctor who is looking at her surprised.

Now, for the first time, she feels embarrassed. Laura, who has wanted to abort with defiant pride, feels ashamed to the bone for having changed her mind. In a soft voice, clumsily, she tries to explain to the doctor, who interrupts her, taking charge of the situation. The assistant goes to look for the nurse, who arrives with Laura's clothing. Laura dresses in the examining room, very quickly. They return her money, the doctor seems suddenly ill-tempered, but polite, and he even wishes her, nicely, good luck. They have her exit through a different door where Gerardo is waiting for her, pale and frightened.

Laura knows she can count on her parents, who will help her, joylessly. At times Gerardo seems happy, at others, desperate. When he's feeling desperate, he disappears for days at a time. When he's happy, he rests his head on her stomach and allows himself to be caressed by Laura, who doesn't know if she loves him.

Laura allows Gerardo and his parents, who moderately hate one another and who at times are accomplices, to decide the date of the wedding, the rental of the apartment, all the details. She immerses herself sleepily in the sensations of her body. During the first months she doesn't have any morning sickness but she sleeps a lot. One weekend they take a trip to Miramar with another couple and Laura sleeps the whole time: on the way there, in the hotel, during the trip home. The others tease her, which she accepts absentmindedly, smiling. Living with Gerardo could end up being difficult, and probably will be later on, when Laura overcomes her indifference which causes her to see herself from afar, as if in a dream.

Until the first three months have passed, Laura fears a miscarriage, her just punishment for having wanted to get rid of the child that she now wants so much. She doesn't run, she doesn't bend over, she sits down carefully, she avoids the stairs. During that time she walks with her torso leaning back, sticking her belly out. From her fourth month on she doesn't have to pretend anymore, the large clothes begin to fit her.

Laura now feels the first movements of the baby, like those of a fish enclosed in a tank that is too small, and in its comings and goings, it gently brushes against the glass walls. She makes Gerardo remain for long minutes with his hand pressed against her belly, and although he claims to feel the little kicks, she is sure he's lying. She trusts her obstetrician, a young doctor with white hair who has a curious repertoire of jokes to make pregnant women laugh. Although sometimes the jokes aren't funny and at times he repeats them, she always laughs politely. Around the sixth month she thinks she feels more contractions than she should. The doctor prescribes Duvadilan and rest.

She doesn't feel impatient, she enjoys her body, she takes long naps, and at night she has insomnia. Toward the end, the joints in her legs begin to ache, especially her knees. Laura has gained more weight than she should and the doctor gently scolds her and puts her on a no-salt diet. Now the baby's movements seem to cause great waves inside her belly, the ebb and flow of liquid that is plainly visible, but that isn't enough for Laura; she likes to place her hands so she can feel it from the outside.

Laura buys diapers and blankets, but she can't decide how to bathe the baby, in a portable bathtub or in the sink. Her doubts keep her awake for several nights; she can't talk about it with Gerardo, who is sick of hearing her arguments for and against the bathtub or the sink.

Her impatience reaches its limit. The last week is almost unbearable; the minutes drag like long yellow worms. One Saturday while dining with Gerardo at his parents' house, she feels the first jab of pain while she's eating some pasta. It's like a small earthquake that shakes her and then passes quickly. She dreads yet wants the next one to come. The pains continue to come sporadically all weekend, and on Sunday night, they come every six minutes. The doctor prescribes an antispasmodic and asks them to call him if they have no effect.

At one in the morning she goes with Gerardo to the hospital, an old building which at that time of night is desolate and gloomy. They give her an injection that helps to eliminate the ineffective contractions, but the process doesn't stop, and now the pain is terrible. Panting doesn't help to control it; screaming is a pleasure. Between contractions, Laura tries futilely to relax, she curls up, tense on the bed, she vomits. The pain, like a cloud, colors her perceptions; everything is pain, and although she tries to cling to the image of her child, she can no longer remember why she is there. At seven in the morning the doctor comes to get her, he calms her down then says good-bye to her, he will see her again in the delivery room.

A nurse helps her to climb up on the gurney. The trip to the delivery room is frightening, the pain becomes more intense by the minute, it never leaves her, and there no longer seems to be a pause between contractions–they are one minute apart.

The doctor is waiting for her in the delivery room; his face is familiar; she can't remember where she has seen him before. His hair is dark; he's not her obstetrician. The pain lessens her surprise, and Laura is already lying on the high table with her legs raised and supported by metal stirrups. It's difficult to understand why they tie her that way, her arms and legs, as if trying to prevent any possibility of her expressing herself. It's not for defense because it's impossible to defend yourself in that position, like a great sea turtle that's been turned on its back so its most vulnerable and delicious parts are left exposed.

The rubber ties dig slightly into her wrists and Laura trusts the anaesthesia. Only when they place the gas mask over her mouth and nose and she begins to breathe in that yellowish color that seems to ascend directly from her nose into her brain, does she discover that she won't sleep, that the gas will only make her drowsy, hinder her movements, separating her body, where the pain will grow, from her will. Her self crouches in a corner of her mind where the sensations arrive sharply, but to which she is no longer able to respond.

Like the pounding of a hammer and a chisel inserted into her flesh, sculpting it, working it from the inside, the pain works its way through the yellowish-green fog enveloping her while Laura attempts to breathe deeply, deeper, attempting without success to dissolve into the gas that enters through her mouth and nose, continuing to hear the distant voices in spite of her efforts not to, until her right hand manages to free itself from the ties that hold it prisoner to the side of the table. She raises her hand in a silent plea, without trying to interfere with the punishment, nor to interrupt it. She can barely compare the blows of the hammer, inserting the chisel deeper and deeper, with that other imagined pain that the other instrument would have produced, the one she never saw nor will ever see, but which is still working there, deep inside, repeating those blows that are already echoing in her ears, carried by her blood.

Someone carries her in their arms and softly deposits her on one of the beds in the adjoining rooms where several women look at her with curiosity, and where others avoid looking at her. Now Laura obediently follows the preestablished steps: lying down, sitting on the bed, sitting in the chair, finally leaving, while the nurse puts in her hand a little slip of xeroxed paper prescribing several hours of rest, doses of tetramiacin, and a special diet.

Gerardo is waiting to accompany her to a friend's house where she'll spend the rest of the day; in the taxi he mechanically strokes her hand; they begin to suspect that they don't love each other.

Mirta Toledo is a native of Argentina who moved to Forth Worth, Texas, in 1990. A graduate of both the Belgrano School of Fine Arts and the Pueyrredón College of Fine Arts in Argentina, she is an accomplished artist who has participated in over seventy art exhibitions throughout the world and has won many awards for her drawing and sculpture. Although Toledo claims that sculpture is her true love, she has a desire to do it all, which is reflected in the variety of works she has produced.

Toledo's move to Texas was a turning point in her career. In Fort Worth she encountered an unfamiliar, diverse, multicultural community. She was unsure about where she would fit in this community and how she should behave in these new surroundings. It was during this time that Toledo stopped painting and sculpting and began to write and draw self-portraits with the intent of finding herself. She has since published several short stories and two novels. Of her writing she says: "I felt the necessity to write because there were so many things that I wanted to express that were impossible to say with sculpture. I believe writing is something magical, something necessary for the soul. When I write, I have no plan; it's as if someone is telling me what to say. Writing is a creative way to express my feelings about living between two cultures: the one I left behind and the new one I want to become a part of, without losing my identity."

"The Hunchback," a story which portrays the cruelty shown to those who are in some way different, allows Toledo to remind us that diversity, no matter how it is manifested, need not be a disadvantage. The protagonist, although physically deformed, does not view herself as such. Rather, her deformity becomes an asset, allowing her to view the world through the eyes of one who feels blessed because she is not like others.

"In Between," Toledo's first short story, clearly shows her feelings of nostalgia for her native country and her search for identity. She compares her native culture with the strangeness of North American society where everyone is in a hurry, where there is little physical contact with others, and where people carry out many daily functions from inside their cars, completely isolated. The story's narrator comes to identify with a homeless woman, a being who is completely isolated, not so unlike many others in this society.

Mirta Toledo is currently completing work on an illustrated and bilingual collection of short stories.

The Hunchback

by Mirta Toledo

"*T*he woman who slashed the world and the man who burned it were my parents," said Griselda Pérez, before putting a bite of ravioli in her mouth.

No one stopped eating, the others and I continued chewing, as if the swiss chard with ricotta cheese had the consistency of molten lead.

We were in the hotel dining room, sitting at a round table, Pipa, the young women, and I, when they brought her in on a stretcher. They put her down so quickly that none of us could say no, you just couldn't do that in such a place. "And that's why I am like I am, Griselda Pérez, at your service," and she extended her hand with slender fingers, crowned by red nails. We all moved the place settings aside and rose up on tiptoe, placing our bodies across the table, rubbing against the plates, to move in her direction.

"Pleased to meet you!" and upon squeezing that cold hand, wrinkled and lifeless, like the foot of a dead chicken, I felt nauseated.

I leaned back, I settled myself in the chair and remained there, looking at her.

Looking at her eyes, without blinking.

Looking deep inside.

Looking hard and straight ahead.

Watching her while keeping my mouth shut and my nostrils widely flared.

Watching her like a prisoner attempting to penetrate her exterior with the only weapon I possessed, to learn more, to find the truth, attempting to guess what the words she had uttered really meant....

She wiped the sauce from her lips, crossed her little yellow hands, and faced me with a look made up of very dark shadows while her eyebrows rose, forming arches of sadness.

But I didn't stop, because my father had trained me in the art of using my eyes like drills to dissect people just like I was doing to her, until a pinch on my right leg caused me to blink and lose ground.

"You'll have to excuse the child," Pipa told her while she kicked me under the table. "She's not rude, just confused."

We spent the days on the beach, with Griselda seated on a wicker chair that the waiters had brought from the hotel especially for her. The chair was tall and shaped like a throne. We stretched out on the sand, and from down there, we could see her little legs dangling in the air, her long red hair, the unequivocal splendor of her hunchback under the sun.

She was irritating, at least for the others, but not because she had a hunchback. What bothered them was that she had that absurd behavior of showing it off naturally, if not proudly. By doing so, she distinguished herself from the others and remained by definition, separated from the group. And although she was there, within the apparent reach of hands, no one could touch her.

At night after dinner, they would carry her out to the little balcony. Around seven o'clock the musicians would arrive and find her there, rocking back and forth to her own rhythm, the sequins on her dress shining in the moonlight.

During the week, gifts began to arrive for her. First, there were flowers at dinner time, later, boxes of bonbons, and three days before we left, the tiara. From a secret admirer, she told us.

The young women and Pipa spoke to one another with a look. They made me dizzy with that mute verbiage that ended with smiles, dead before they were born, committing suicide right then and there in the corners of their mouths.

On the last night, the photographer arrived and Griselda asked me to help her. I approached her fearfully, but I grabbed her right on her hump to lift her up and put her down in the chair. She smelled like my catechism book, and she even had that mother-of-pearl color that I associated with mysticism.

I couldn't resist the temptation, my fingers got away from me, and I touched her without permission, while my eyes watched my hand without missing a single detail.

It was cold and smooth like glass, and left a sensation of irreality on my fingertips, as if we were all a lie, a farce, or completely nonexistent. It seemed to me that the world's secrets were enclosed inside, that the entire universe was an enormous hump and that life would be much simpler if we all had a visible defect on our backs.

"When you find yours, don't hide it," she told me happily, because at last she was equal to us in stature.

With the passing of the years, I have asked myself who is burdened by whom. Because in the spring the hump blooms, like everything else, and then, of course, it's easier for me. But the winters are difficult, and I can't tolerate the hump, especially when it crushes me, keeping me from being seen.

It scares me!

I begin to disappear...

And when I think that I'm dying, I take the picture out of the box... In their little tailored suits, standing as they should, are the young women. And at my side, with the little crown sunk into her forehead and the lamé butterfly on her breast, Griselda smiles at me, suspended in the air by the power of her hump.

In Between

by Mirta Toledo

I don't know if she sleeps there under the bench, because after six o'clock in the evening I don't go out for anything. Besides, even if I did, there are no street lights, so it would be very difficult to see if she's there.

I see her every morning when I take the kids to school. She's small and somewhat attractive, and is always clinging to that black purse. She reminds me of my aunt Angela, because she has something like an aura of dignity surrounding her. It's precisely because I was looking at that aura that I became distracted and someone honked at me, a rarity in these parts.

What caused her to live this way? I don't know…What must she be feeling so isolated from all human contact? Because here, there are nothing but cars. Vehicles of all types that come and go, that pass by without stopping near her. How strange this society is that they call "mobile"! The word comes from automobile, no doubt…One car for every person, and garages filled with vehicles that come and go, that pass by one another without ever touching.

When I arrived in this city, I didn't understand anything. It seemed deserted, with its lonely streets without sidewalks. But of course, why should there be sidewalks if no one ever walks! I couldn't get over my surprise, and what's worse, I continually expressed it. Someone explained to me about it being a mobile society and then, of course, I said no more.

"Is she crazy, Mommy?" Angel asked me when he saw her more than once.

"Only abandoned," I always answer, not taking my eyes off her as she dusts the bench, or kicks the stones that surround her, or pulls up the grass that grows around her feet in the spring.

"Then why does she live like that, in the street?" asked Santiago, thinking it over with anguish.

"Because she doesn't have a car," I tell him, very sure of myself.

I go out everyday because I have to, but here, going out is also different. I go from the back patio directly to the car, and once inside, to the street. You don't have to put up with storms, much less get wet accidently, and don't even think about being caressed by autumn leaves. No, there's none of that.

I always feel certain that I won't run into anyone, that fictitious idea of turning a corner and coming across a familiar face has become a lie for me.

I adjust my seat belt because I've grown to like speed, and then I turn on some music, no longer just for pleasure, but to feel companionship.

Latinos in the United States
We are almost a Nation...

Everyday I go through the same routine: before eight o'clock I take the kids to school and then I drop my husband off at work. I say good-bye to all three without getting out of the car; perhaps it's because there inside, our kisses seem more intimate.

We came from native America
descendants of Blacks and Spaniards...

Sometimes I do get out of the car, like when I go to the supermarket, or to a bookstore to see what's new or to see if they have anything to say about "down there," about my Argentina.

In our migrant minds
Sometimes there is confusion...

Other times I go to the library. And of course, to the post office, which continues to be a sacred meeting place, despite the letters that don't arrive.

Don't let them convince you
Don't lose your Spanish language...

When I leave each place, our little blue car is always waiting for me. I no longer know what I'd do without it, because as soon as I turn the key, the voice of Celia Cruz embraces me, and continues to sing to me:

Latin America, you live within me
I want this message
to reach you...

Invariably I return home around ten o'clock in the morning. And although I have several ways to choose from, whenever I can, I go by Trail Lake to see the woman on the bench. I feel there is something that unites us, besides the curiosity that she provokes in me with her black purse and the fact that she never lets loose of it.

"What do you suppose she has inside, Mommy?" my children ask, because they're at the age when they still believe I know everything.

"It intrigues me, too," I tell them. "She holds on to it so fiercely!"

When I get out of the car, I lock it, and then I'm "safe and sound" on the back patio, then in the house. I fix myself a cup of coffee and go into the little back room, the place where I work.

"This room could be in China, in Italy, in Australia, or in Japan!" my husband once commented. "Wherever, it's the same, because this place is you. This room isn't here, but in Buenos Aires..."

It's true, I admit it. And what's more, everyday it becomes more evident. But then, where am I, if not here, or there?

"In between, Mommy! In English they say 'in between.'"

Yes, in between, as far from Fort Worth as from Buenos Aires, so anchored in between that I don't know how to jump to either side. Will this be my final place? In between...

And the letters that don't arrive. It's because they don't write, because for my family and friends I'm simply absent, a memory that no longer belongs to Buenos Aires, a stranger who speaks English and lives in a "First World" country. But for me, they are a continual presence, ghosts of true affections, those who speak my language, the only ones who can truly know me: those who dream my dreams.

I filled my suitcases with the memories of my loved ones when I left, the same suitcases I carried through customs and airports every time we moved to a new city.

"Throw something away, Mommy," my children innocently told me. But not me, I held on even tighter to those heavy suitcases.

"Hey! Are you going to tell me you can't get rid of something?" said my husband, who likes to travel light. "Think about it," he complained. "What use is all that stuff you're carrying in there? So many years have gone by." And I answer him with my hands turned into claws, and with my family and friends, always traveling with me without knowing it, there inside my suitcases.

"Do you suppose she has some treasure in her purse, Mommy?" they asked me yesterday when they saw her.

"Yes, kids. And in Spanish we call them 'memories.'"

Publications by Gloria Artigas

Short Story Collections

"El peñón de la viuda" y otros cuentos. Santo Domingo: Editorial Gaviotas, 1988.

Relatos de mar y tierra. Santo Domingo, n. p., 1990.

Encuentros y desencuentros. Santo Domingo: Editorial Gaviotas, 1991.

Bellamar. Chile: Municipalidad de San Antonio, 1992.

Short Stories

"Desde el fondo de ti y arrodillado." In *Sustantivo...Cuentos, Adjetivo... Premiados, Género... Mujeres.* Ed. Asociación de Mujeres de Negocios y Profesionales Santiago: Editorial Montegrande, 1991. 61-62. (Winner of second place in the Primer Concurso de Mujeres de Habla Hispana).

"Rincones de humo." In *Sustantivo...Cuentos, Adjetivo...Premiados, Género...Mujeres,* Ed. Asociación de Mujeres de Negocios y Profesionales de Santiago: Editorial Montegrande, 1991. La Noria, 1993. 49-55.

Publications by Yolanda Bedregal

Novels

Bajo el oscuro sol. La Paz: Editorial Los Amigos del Libro, 1971. (Winner of the Premio Nacional de Novela "Erich Guttentag").

Short Story Collections

Naufragio. 2nd edition. La Paz: Librería Editorial Juventud, 1977.

Escrito. Quito: Printer Graphic, 1994. (Poetry and short stories).

Poetry

Nadir. La Paz: Empresa Editora Universo, 1950.

Del mar y la ceniza. Alegatos. Antología. La Paz: Biblioteca Paceña, 1957.

Antología mínima. La Paz: Editorial El Siglo, 1968.

Almadía. 2nd edition. La Paz: Librería Editorial Juventud, 1977.

Ecos. 2nd edition. La Paz: Librería Editorial Juventud, 1977.

Poemar. 2nd edition. La Paz: Librería Editorial Juventud, 1977.

El cántaro del angelito. La Paz: n.p., 1979. (Poetry for children).

Convocatorias. Ecuador: Artes Gráficas Señal Impreseñal, 1994.

Escrito. Quito: Printer Graphic, 1994. (Poetry and short stories).

Short Stories

"Peregrina." In *Cuentistas paceños.* Ed. Raúl Botelho Gosálvez. La Paz: Ediciones Casa de la Cultura, 1988. 175-180.

"De como Milinco huyó de la escuela." *Antología del cuento boliviano.* Ed. Armando Soriano Badani. La Paz: Editorial Los Amigos del Libro, 1991. 119-122.

Works Translated into English

"Good Evening, Agatha." In *Landscapes of a New Land: Short Fiction by Latin American Women.* Ed. Marjorie Agosín. Fredonia, New York: White Pine Press, 1989. 27-30.

"The Traveler." In *Fire from the Andes: Short Fiction by Women from Bolivia, Ecuador, and Peru.* Eds. Susan E. Benner and Kathy S. Leonard. Albuquerque: University of New Mexico Press, 1997.

Other

Calendario folklórico del Departamento de La Paz. (With Antonio González Bravo). La Paz: Dirección General de Cultura, 1956.

Poesía de Bolivia, de la época precolombina al modernismo. Selected and presented by Yolanda Bedregal. Buenos Aires: Editorial Universitaria de Buenos Aires, 1964. (This work includes over 300 authors).

Antología de la poesía boliviana. La Paz: Editorial Los Amigos del Libro, 1977. (Encyclopedia of Bolivian poetry from pre-republican and pre-colonial times).

Ayllú: el altiplano boliviano. (Text by Yolanda Bedregal, photographs by Peter McFarren). La Paz: Museo Nacional de Etnografía y Folklore and Editorial Los Amigos del Libro, 1984.

Articles on the author

Agosín, Marjorie. "Para un retrato de Yolanda Bedregal." *Revista Iberoamericana* 134 (January–March, 1986): 267-270.

Weldon, Alice. "In Reference to the National Revolution of Bolivia: Three Novels by Women." Diss., University of Maryland, 1996.

Publications by Velia Calvimontes

Short Story Collections

*Y el mundo sigue girando...*La Paz: Editora Talleres Gráficos Rocabado, 1975.

Rinconcuentos. Cochabamba: Talleres Gráficos Poligraf, 1988.

Abre la tapa y destapa un cuento. Cochabamba: Honorable Municipalidad de Cochabamba Talleres Gráficos H & P, 1991.

La ronda de los niños. Cochabamba: Editorial Vendilusiones, 1991.

De la tierra y de las preguntas. (With Blanca Garnica). Cochabamba: Colorgraf Rodríguez, 1992.

Babirusa y sus cuentos del Tawantinsuyu. Cochabamba: Editora H & P, 1993.

El uniforme. Cochabamba: Editora H & P, 1993.
Amigo de papel (diario de un adolescente). Cochabamba: Colorgraf, 1995.
Babirusa te cuento de cómo...? Cochabamba: Colorgraf, 1995.
En la piel morena de Babirusa. Cochabamba: Colorgraf, 1995.
Lágrimas y risas. Cochambamba: Colorgraf Rodríguez, 1995.
Cuentos de los duendes de la luna. Cochabamba: Ediciones T'ikallajta, 1996.

Poetry

Gotas de rocío: Poemas para los más pequeñitos. Cochabamba: Ediciones
   T'ikallajta, 1995.

Short Stories

"El regalo de navidad." In *Primera antología: prosa.* Cochabamba: Unión
   Nacional de Poetas y Escritores de Cochabamba, 1994. 87-89.

Publications by Sylvia Diez Fierro

Short Story Collections

Pulsos Cardinales. (With María Eliana Carrasco Linford, Tatiana Fáez
   Sotomayor, and María Isabel Riquelme Romero). Chile: Ediciones
   Pentagrama, 1995.

Short Stories

"La esposa del marino." In *Sustantivo...Cuentos, Adjetivo...Premiados,
   Género...Mujeres.* Ed. Federación Nacional de Mujeres de Negocios y
   Profesionales de Chile. Santiago: Editorial La Noria, 1993. 75-82.

Publications by Inés Fernández Moreno

Short Story Collections

La vida en la cornisa. Buenos Aires: Emecé Editores, 1993.
Efectos secundarios. Buenos Aires: Emecé Editores, 1996.

Short Stories

"Madre para armar." In *Antología "Cuentos de La Felguera 1956-1993."*
   Spain: Edición de la Caja de Asturias y la Sociedad de Festejos San
   Pedro de La Felguera, 1994.

Publications by Gilda Holst Molestina

Short Story Collections

Más sin nombre que nunca. Quito: Casa de la Cultura Ecuatoriana, Núcleo
   del Guayas, Banco Central del Ecuador, 1989.
Turba de signos. Quito: abrapalabra editores, 1989.

Short Stories

"El mar sigue azul," "Por una mirada," and "Un lugar limitado. In *El lugar de las palabras.* Guayaquil: Banco Central del Ecuador, 1986. 51-59.
"Mas sin nombre que nunca." *Revista Qlisgen* 7.12 (1987).
"Debo a las novelas." *Hispamérica 48* (1988): 96-101.
"Una palpitación detrás de los ojos." In *El muro y la intemperie.* Ed. Julio Ortega. Hanover New Hampshire: Ediciones del Norte, 1989. 51-54.
"Las albarradas: Los últimos aguadores de Muey." In *El libro de los abuelos.* Ecuador: Fundación Pedro Vicente Maldonado y Casa de la Cultura, Núcleo de Guayas, 1990. 128-134.
"Luisa Paijos." In *Así en la tierra como en los sueños. Cuentos escogidos.* Ed. Mario Campaña Avilés. Quito: Editorial El Conejo, 1991. 150-153.
"Palabreo." In *!A que sí!* Eds. V. García Serrano, A. Grant Cash, and C. de la Torre. Boston: Heinle & Heinle Publishers, 1993. 256-257.
"Palabreo." In *Cuento contigo.* Ed. Cecilia Ansaldo Briones. Quito: Universidad Católica de Santiago de Guayaquil, Universidad Andina Simón Bolívar, Subsede Quito, 1993. 311.
"Reunión." *Revista Imagen* Mar. 1994.

Publications by María Eugenia Lorenzini

Novel

Después de ayer. Santiago: Editorial Hilo Negro, 1994.

Short Stories

"Paradero del bus No. 46." In *Sustantivo...Cuentos, Adjetivo...Premiados, Género...Mujeres.* Ed. Federacion Nacional de Mujeres de Negocios y Profesionales de Chile. Santiago: Editorial Montegrande, 1991. 55-57.

Publications by Andrea Maturana

Short Story Collections

(Des) Encuentros, (Des) Esperados. Chile: Editorial de los Andes, 1992.

Short Stories

"Maletas." In *Antología Fempress: El cuento feminista latinoamericano.* Eds. Adriana Santa Cruz and Viviana Erazo. Santiago: Fempress, 1988. 21-22.
"Canción de cuna." In *Brevísima relación del cuento breve de Chile.* Ed. Juan Epple. Santiago: Ediciones LAR, 1989. 91-92.

Publications by Viviana Mellet

Short Story Collections

La mujer alada. Lima: Peisa, 1994.

Short Stories

"El buen aire de la noche." In *La tentación de escribir.* Lima: Ediciones Flora Tristán, 1993. 37-43.

Publications by Ana María Shua

Novels

Soy Paciente. Buenos Aires: Losada, 1980. (Awarded first prize in the International Contest of Narrative by the publisher Losada. Made into a movie by Rodolfo Corral).

Los amores de Laurita. Buenos Aires: Sudamericana, 1984. (Made into a movie by Antonio Ottone).

El libro de los recuerdos. Buenos Aires: Sudamericana, 1994.

Short Story Collections

La sueñera. Buenos Aires: Minotauro, 1984.

Viajando se conoce gente. Buenos Aires: Sudamericana, 1988. (Awarded first prize in the Primer Concurso de Cuentos Eróticos de la *Revista Don).*

Casa de geishas. Buenos Aires: Sudamericana, 1992.

Short Stories

"Fiestita con animación" and "La sala del piano." In *Hispamérica 15*.45 (1986): 157-163.

"Fiestita con animación." In *El muro y la intemperie.* Ed. Julio Ortega. Hanover, New Hampshire: Ediciones del Norte, 1989. 83-85.

"Fishing Days." In *Secret Weavers: Stories of the Fantastic by Women of Argentina and Chile.* Ed. Marjorie Agosín. Fredonia, New York: White Pine Press, 1992. 157-163.

"Other/Other." In *Secret Weavers: Stories of the Fantastic by Women of Argentina and Chile.* Ed. Marjorie Agosín. Fredonia, New York: White Pine Press, 1992. 146-156.

"Cirugía menor." In *Una antología de nueva ficción argentina.* Ed. Juan Forn. Barcelona: Editorial Anagrama, 1993. 121-128.

Poetry

El sol y yo. Buenos Aires: Ediciones Pro, 1967. (Awarded the prize Fondo Nacional de las Artes, Faja de Honor de la Sociedad Argentina de Escritores).

Children's Literature

La batalla de los elefantes y los cocodriles. Buenos Aires: Sudamericana, 1988.

Expedición al Amazonas. Buenos Aires: Sudamericana, 1988.

La fábrica del terror. Buenos Aires: Sudamericana, 1990. (Awarded Premio Lista de Honor de ALIJU and Premio Banco del Libro de Venezuela).

La puerta para salir del mundo. Buenos Aires: Sudamericana, 1992.

Cuentos de judíos con fantasmas y demonios. Buenos Aires: Grupo Editorial Shalom, 1994.

Humorous Essays

El marido argentino promedio. Buenos Aires: Sudamericana, 1991.

Risas y emociones de la cocina judía. Buenos Aires: Grupo Editorial Shalom, 1993.

Articles on the author

de Miguel, María Esther. "Cuando la realidad se hace absurdo." *El Cronista Comercial* Oct. 1980.

Zapata, Marcel. "Eficaz novela de humor negro." *Diario Convicción* July 1981.

Pollock, Beth. "Los amores de Laurita." (Review). *Chasqui* 21.1 (1992): 166-168.

Pollock, Beth. "El marido argentino promedio." (Review). *Chasqui* 22.1 (1993): 105-107.

Domínguez, Nora. "Barrio Norte, primavera de 1994, Ana María Shua." *The Buenos Aires Review* Sept. 1994: 6-7.

Fernández de Tujague, Silvia. "El recuerdo es dudoso." *La Capital* Nov. 1994.

Pollock, Beth. "Ana María Shua." *Hispamérica* 23.69 (1994): 45-54.

Torres, Angel. "Retrato de familia." *El Día* Sept. 1994: 4.

Publications by Mirta Toledo

Novel

La semilla elemental. Buenos Aires: Editorial Vinciguerra, 1993.

Short Stories

"In Between." *Napenay* 14 (1992): 45-46.

"El amante." *Opinión Cultural* Mar.-Apr. 1992.

"Jacinto." *El Grillo: Revista de Cultura* Apr.-May 1993: 22-24.

"Jacinto." *Relatos de mujeres: I Antología.* Madrid: Ediciones Torremozas, S.L., 1994. 77-81.

"Papelitos mágicos." *Letras femeninas* 20.1-2 (1995): 233-235.

Agosín, Marjorie, ed. *Happiness: Stories by Marjorie Agosín*. Fredonia, New York: White Pine Press, 1993.

———. *Landscapes of a New Land: Short Fiction by Latin American Women*. Fredonia, New York: White Pine Press, 1993.

Ahern, Maureen, ed. *A Rosario Castellanos Reader*. Austin: University of Texas Press, 1988.

Alegría, Claribel. *Family Album*. Willimantic, Connecticut: Curbstone Press, 1991.

———. *Luisa in Realityland*. Willimantic: Curbstone Press, 1987.

Allende, Isabel. *The Stories of Eva Luna*. New York: Atheneum, 1991.

Allgood, Marilyn, ed. *Another Way to Be: Selected Works of Rosario Castellanos*. Athens: The University of Georgia Press, 1990.

Arkin, Marian, and Barbara Shollar, eds. *Longman Anthology of Literature by Women, 1875-1975*. New York: Longman, 1989.

Arredondo, Inés. *Underground River and Other Stories*. Lincoln: University of Nebraska, 1996.

Barros, Pía. *Transitory Fears*. Santiago: Asterión Publishers, 1989.

Benner, Susan and Kathy S. Leonard, eds. *Fire from the Andes: Short Fiction by Women from Bolivia, Ecuador, and Peru*. Albuquerque: University of New Mexico Press, 1997.

Bombal, María Luisa. *New Islands and Other Stories*. New York: Farrar, Straus & Giroux, 1982; Ithaca: Cornell University Press, 1988.

Boyce Davies, Carole, and 'Molara Ogundipe-Leslie, eds. *Moving Beyond Boundaries. Volume 1: International Dimensions of Black Women's Writing*. New York: New York University Press, 1995.

Boza, María del Carmen, Beverly Silva, and Carmen Valle, eds. *Nosotras: Latina Literature Today*. Tempe, Arizona: Bilingual Review/Press, 1986.

Braschi, Giannina. *Empire of Dreams*. New Haven and London: Yale University Press, 1994.

Campobello, Nellie. *Cartucho* and *My Mother's Hands*. Austin: University of Texas Press, 1988.

Campos, Julieta. *Celina or the Cats*. Pittsburgh: Latin Amercian Literary Review Press, 1995.

Castellanos, Rosario. *City of Kings*. Pittsburgh: Latin American Literary Review Press, 1992.

Castro-Klarén, Sara, and Sylvia Molloy, eds. *Women's Writing in Latin America: An Anthology*. Boulder: Westview Press, 1991.

Chávez-Vásquez, Gloria. *Opus Americanus: Short Stories.* United States: White Owl Editions, 1993.

Correas de Zapata, Celia, ed. *Short Stories by Latin American Women: The Magic and the Real.* Houston: Arte Público Press, 1990.

de Vallbona, Rima. *Flowering Inferno: Tales of Sinking Hearts.* Pittsburgh: Latin American Literary Review Press, 1994.

di Giovanni, Norman Thomas, and Susan Ashe, eds. *Celeste Goes Dancing and Other Stories.* San Francisco: North Point Press, 1990.

Erro-Peralta, Nora, and Caridad Silva-Nuñez, eds. *Beyond the Border: A New Age in Latin American Women's Fiction.* Pittsburgh: Cleis Press, 1991.

Esteves, Carmen C., and Lizabeth Paravisini-Gebert, eds. *Green Candy and Juicy Flotsam: Short Stories by Caribbean Women.* New Brunswick: Rutgers University Press, 1991.

Fagundes Telles, Lygia. *Tigrela and Other Stories.* New York: Avon Books, 1986.

Fernández, Roberta, ed. *In Other Words: Literature by Latinas of the United States.* Houston: Arte Público Press, 1994.

Fernández Olmos, Margarite, and Lizabeth Paravisini-Gebert, eds. *Pleasure in the Word: Erotic Writing by Latin American Women.* Fredonia, New York: White Pine Press, 1994.

——, eds. *Remaking a Lost Harmony: Stories from the Hispanic Caribbean.* Fredonia, New York: White Pine Press, 1995.

Ferré, Rosario. *Sweet Diamond Dust: A Novel and Three Stories of Life in Puerto Rico.* New York: Ballantine Books, 1988.

——. *The Youngest Doll.* Lincoln: University of Nebraska Press, 1991.

Gómez, Alma, Cherrie Moraga, and Mariana Romo-Carmona, eds. *Cuentos: Stories by Latinas.* New York: Kitchen Table, Women of Color Press, 1983.

Graziano, Frank, ed. *Alejandra Pizarnik: A Profile.* Durango: Logbridge-Rhodes, Inc., 1987.

Heker, Liliana. *The Stolen Party and Other Stories.* Toronto: Coach House Press, 1994.

Jaramillo, Enrique Levi, ed. *When New Flowers Bloomed: Short Stories by Women Writers from Costa Rica and Panama.* Pittsburgh: Latin American Literary Review Press, 1991.

Lewald, Ernest, ed. *The Web: Stories by Argentine Women.* Washington D.C: Three Continents Press, 1983.

Lispector, Clarice. *Family Ties.* Austin: University of Texas Press, 1972.

——. *The Foreign Legion: Stories and Chronicles.* Manchester: Carcanet, 1986; New York: New Directions, 1992.

——. *Soulstorm: Stories.* New York: New Directions Publications, 1989.

Mallet, Marilú. *Voyage to the Other Extreme: Five Stories.* Montreal: Vehicule, 1985.

Manguel, Alberto, ed. *Other Fires: Short Fiction by Latin American Women.* New York: Clarkson N. Potter Publishers, Inc., 1986.

Meyer, Doris, and Margarita Fernández Olmos, eds. *Contemporary Women Authors of Latin America: New Translations.* Brooklyn: Brooklyn College Press, 1983.

Milligan, Bryce, Mary Guerrero Milligan, and Angela de Hoyos, eds. *Daughters of the Fifth Sun: A Collection of Latina Fiction and Poetry.* New York: Riverhead Books, 1995.

Mistral, Gabriela. *Crickets and Frogs: A Fable.* New York: Atheneum, 1972.

———. *The Elephant and His Secret: Based on a Fable by Gabriela Mistral.* New York: Antheneum, 1974. (Bilingual, children's literature).

Mordecai, Pamela, and Betty Wilson, eds. *Her True-True Name: An Anthology of Women's Writing from the Caribbean.* Oxford: Heinemann, 1989.

Muñiz Huberman, Angelina. *Enclosed Garden.* Pittsburgh: Latin American Literary Review Press, 1988.

Naranjo, Carmen. *There Never Was a Once Upon a Time.* Pittsburgh: Latin American Literary Review Press, 1989.

Niggli, Josephina. *Mexican Village.* Albuquerque: University of New Mexico Press, 1994.

Ocampo, Silvina. *Leopoldina's Dream.* London and New York: Penguin, 1988.

O'hara, Maricarmen. *Cuentos para todos/Tales for Everybody.* Ventura: Alegría Hispana Publications, 1994.

Partnoy, Alicia. *The Little School: Tales of Disappearance and Survival in Argentina.* San Francisco: Cleis Press, 1986.

———, ed. *You Can't Drown the Fire: Latin American Women Writing in Exile.* San Francisco: Cleis Press, 1988.

Pereira, Teresinha. *Help, I'm Drowning.* Chicago: Palos Heights Press, 1975.

Peri Rossi, Cristina. *A Forbidden Passion.* San Francisco: Cleis Press, 1993.

Picon Garfield, Evelyn, ed. *Women's Fiction from Latin America: Selections from Twelve Contemporary Authors.* Detroit: Wayne State University Press, 1988.

Poey, Delia, ed. *Out of the Mirrored Garden: New Fiction by Latin American Women.* New York: Anchor Books, 1996.

Ross, Kathleen, and Yvette Miller. eds. *Scents of Wood and Silence: Short Stories by Latin American Women Writers.* Pittsburgh: Latin American Literary Review Press, 1991.

Sadlier, Darlene J., ed. *Brazilian Women Writing.* Bloomington: Indiana University Press, 1992.

———. *One Hundred Years After Tomorrow: Brazilian Women's Fiction in the 20th Century.* Bloomington: Indiana University Press, 1992.

Urbano, Victoria, ed. *Five Women Writers of Costa Rica: Short Stories by Carmen Naranjo, Eunice Odio, Yolanda Oreamuno, Victoria Urbano, and Rima Vallbona.* Beaumont: Asociación de Literatura Femenina Hispánica, 1978.

Valenzuela, Luisa. *Clara: Thirteen Short Stories and a Novel.* New York: Harcourt Brace Jovanovich, 1976.

———. *Open Door.* San Francisco: North Point Press, 1988.

———. *Other Weapons.* Hanover, New Hampshire: Ediciones del Norte, 1985.

———. *Strange Things Happen Here: 26 Short Stories and a Novel.* New York: Harcourt Brace Jovanovich, 1979.

———. *The Censors: A Bilingual Selection of Stories.* Willimantic, Connecticut: Curbstone Press, 1988.

Van Steen, Edla, ed. *A Bag of Stories.* Pittsburgh: Latin American Literary Review Press, 1991.

Vega, Ana Lydia. *True and False Romances: Stories and a Novella.* London: Serpent's Tail, 1994.

Vélez, Diana, ed. *Reclaiming Medusa: Short Stories by Contemporary Puerto Rican Women.* Spinsters/Aunt Lute Book Co., 1988.

Vigil, Evangelina, ed. *Woman of Her Word: Hispanic Women Write.* Houston: Arte Público Press, 1987.

Other Useful Sources

Alarcon, Norma, and Sylvia Kossnar. *Bibliography of Hispanic Women Writers.* Bloomington: Chicano-Riqueño Studies, 1980.

Balderston, Daniel. *The Latin American Short Story: An Annotated Guide to Anthologies and Criticism.* New York: Greenwood Press, 1992.

Corvalán, Graciela. *Latin American Women in English Translation: A Bibliography.* Los Angeles: Latin American Studies Center, 1980.

Freudenthal, Juan R., and Patricia M. Freudenthal, eds. *Index to Anthologies of Latin American Literature in English Translation.* Boston: G.K. Hall and Co., 1977.

Fundação Biblioteca Nacional, Ministerio da Cultura. *Brazilian Authors Translated Abroad.* Rio de Janeiro: n. p., 1994.

Hulet, Claude L., ed. *Latin American Prose in English Translation. A Bibliography.* Washington, D.C: Pan American Union, 1964

Kanellos Nicolás, ed. *Biographical Dictionary of Hispanic Literature in the United States: The Literature of Puerto Ricans, Cuban Americans, and Other Hispanic Writers.* New York: Greenwood Press, 1989.

Leonard, Kathy S., ed. *Index to Translated Short Fiction by Latin American Women in English Languate Anthologies.* Westport: Greenwood Press. (Forthcoming)

Levine, Suzanne Jill. *Latin American Fiction and Poetry in Translation.* New York: Center for Inter-American Relations, 1970.

Marting, Diane, ed. *Spanish American Women Writers: A Bio-bibliographic Source Book.* New York: Greenwood Press, 1990.

———. *Women Writers of Spanish America: An Annotated Bio-bibliographic Guide.* New York: Greenwood Press, 1987.

Resnick, Margery, and Isabelle de Courtivron, eds. *Women Writers in Translation. An Annotated Bibliography, 1945-1982.* New York and London: Garland Publishing, Inc., 1984.

Shaw, Bradley A., ed. *Latin American Literature in English Translation. An Annotated Bibliography.* New York: New York University Press, 1976.

Stern, Irwin, ed. *Dictionary of Brazilian Literature.* New York: Greenwood Press, 1988.

Wilson, Jason, ed. *An A to Z of Modern Latin American Literature in English Translation.* London: The Institute of Latin American Studies, 1989.

Compiled by Kathy S. Leonard

Notes on the Editor/Translator

Kathy Leonard received her Ph.D. in Hispanic Linguistics from the University of California, Davis, and is currently an associate professor of Spanish at Iowa State University in Ames. She has published translations of short stories by Latin American women writers in a number of journals, including *Feminist Studies, The Antigonish Review, Michigan Quarterly Review, Critical Matrix: The Princeton Journal of Women, Gender, and Culture, Puerto del Sol,* and *Flyway: A Literary Review.* Her co-edited and translated volume of short stories titled *Fire from the Andes: Short Fiction by Women from Bolivia, Ecuador, and Peru* will be published by the University of New Mexico Press in 1997. Leonard is a 1998 Fulbright Scholar to Bolivia where she will complete a volume of interviews with Bolivian women authors.